Emperor

Roderick Donatus

Published by Prince of Spires, 2020.

This is a work of fiction. Similarities to real people, places, or events are entirely coincidental.

EMPEROR

First edition. December 4, 2020.

Written by Roderick Donatus.

Also by Roderick Donatus

Emperor

Watch for more at https://www.roderickdonatus.com/.

To my wife.

Because you inspire me and you let me write.

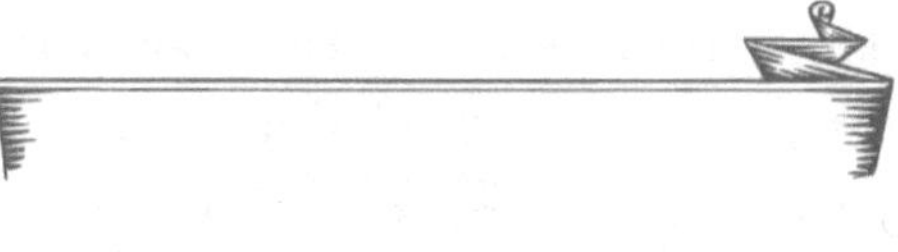

Problems

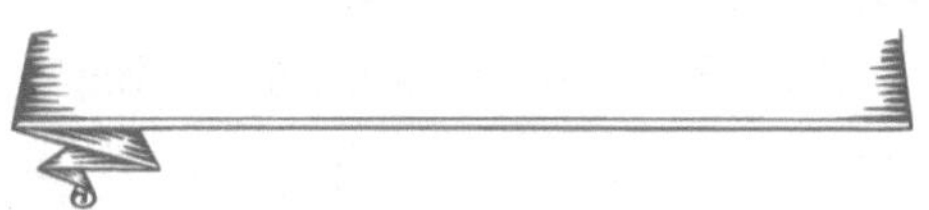

Shiro had to hurry to keep up with Master Chin's long strides. Shiro was definitely in trouble. He followed Master Chin through the broad corridors of the palace, walking past a mural depicting the final victory of the first emperor which had led to the founding of the Empire. The masked image of the emperor stared down at him in judgment. Shiro averted his gaze.

The master had only told him to follow. Someone must have found out about the mistake. Maybe he could explain. He had been so sure that his calculations had been correct. And normally Taizo double-checked them. But Taizo had been ill that day. And then there had been the emergency, so he had had to rush it through. But it had been an honest mistake.

They took a left turn. Shiro wasn't sure anymore where they were. He'd been too focused on Master Chin's shoes to keep up. There were more guards around this section of the palace. Where was he being taken? He had assumed that he would be taken to the head of the trade department. But they would have already reached there. It could only mean he was being taken to someone higher up.

They took another turn and walked through a door. Shiro found himself outside. He raised his arm in front of his face against the glare of the morning sun and saw that he was standing in the central square of the Forbidden City. Master Chin was already partway across the square and making straight for the Imperial Quarter. Shiro had to run to catch up, his robe billowing around him.

There could be only one reason he was being taken to the Imperial Quarter – to be questioned by one of the Ministers of State who had their offices close to the emperor. They wouldn't worry themselves about someone like him, would they? He was only a clerk in the trade department, working on distributing rice through the empire. The mistake must have been even worse than he'd thought, for it to come to one of the Minister's attention. Maybe he wouldn't just be expelled. Would they flog him for this mistake? How would he face his family after such a disgrace?

They walked up the stairs to the main entrance. Two guards holding tall halberds stood on either side of the bronze doors, their black uniforms in sharp contrast with the red and green of the woodwork behind them. They were admitted without so much as a glance.

The atrium of the Imperial Quarter spread out in front of them. Shiro took a moment to admire the view, despite his worries. He had been here only once before, on the day he had been admitted into the Imperial administration four years ago. The atrium was easily sixty feet across. The red pillars supporting the roof were so broad that they must have been cut from hundred-year-old oak trees. Bronze reliefs decorated the walls, and several statues lined the atrium. Straight ahead were the double doors that ran from floor to ceiling, through which one would enter the throne room. He had only heard stories about how lavishly that room was decorated.

He followed Master Chin to the right - to Grandmaster Dalip's office. If he was being taken there, then even a flogging would be merciful.

Master Chin gave a polite knock on the door. "Enter," a warm voice from inside the room said.

Master Chin opened the door and stepped back. He waved Shiro through and Shiro walked in. The door closed behind him with an ominous thud.

Ahead, Grandmaster Dalip, dressed in a red silk gown decorated with a golden crane bird, sat behind an ornate ebony desk bent over a stack of papers. The light shining through the windows in the opposite wall reflected in the polished surface of the desk. Grandmaster Dalip ignored Shiro. The streaks of grey in his hair and moustache, which framed a long face, gave the man a regal look.

Shiro had only once been this close to the grandmaster before. Half a year ago, the grandmaster had visited the trade department and had stopped by Shiro's desk and complimented Shiro on a report he'd done on the expected rice harvest and the best ways to distribute it through the different provinces. Shiro had bragged about it to his friend Taizo for a week.

The silence lengthened. Beads of sweat rolled from Shiro's brow. His stomach cramped as he tried not to fidget with his hands and he said a quick prayer that he would not throw up in front of Grandmaster Dalip.

The room could have held twenty people, but at the moment Shiro and Grandmaster Dalip were alone. A jade sword, four feet long, hung on the wall behind the grandmaster. A large bookcase covered one complete wall. A painting showing angels coming to the aid of the first emperor hung on the opposite wall.

Finally, Grandmaster Dalip looked up. "We have a problem." He had a melodious voice. "You must understand that this is coming from the emperor himself."

Shiro fell to his knees. "I'm sorry, Grandmaster," He blurted out. "Taizo was ill that day. And then we had to rush it through."

Grandmaster Dalip gave him a look of surprise. "What are you talking about?"

"My mistakes in the calculations for the grain shipments to Dashi province. They were an honest mistake. I didn't mean to send too much."

"Get up. I have bigger things to worry about than some calculation mistake from a clerk. In fact, I have the perfect way for you to make amends." Grandmaster Dalip beckoned him closer.

Shiro was at a loss for words. He wouldn't be flogged, and he wouldn't be expelled. But then why was he here? He got up and walked over to the desk.

"As I was about to say," Grandmaster Dalip continued, "the peace talks with the delegation from the Khaganate are scheduled for tonight. It is imperative that they succeed so we can end the unrest on our western border. We are close to signing a treaty." Grandmaster Dalip placed his hand on the documents he had been working on when Shiro had entered. "The final round of the negotiations have to be overseen by the emperor himself. The Khaganate expects him there as a sign that they are being taken seriously. Any lapse in the proper forms will be taken as an insult."

Shiro found himself nodding. The war with the Khaganate had been taking its toll on the western provinces. The shipment of supplies that contained his error had been sent to support the war effort in the Dashi province.

"However"-Grandmaster Dalip raised his hand-"we have a problem. Just this night, the emperor has fallen ill. He is unable to leave his bed chamber, let alone preside over negotiations with a foreign nation."

Shiro raised a hand to his mouth. "Will the emperor be all right?"

"Yes, yes. His Holiness will recover just fine. That's not why you are here. We require your service."

"Of course, Grandmaster. I will do anything." He would do whatever it took to aid his emperor and serve the empire. It was why he had chosen to enter into the imperial bureaucracy.

"I expected nothing less. We have been following you for a while now, and you are an exceptional asset to the imperial bureaucracy. Which is why we now need your assistance." Grandmaster Dalip paused for a breath. "You need to stand in for the emperor tonight during the negotiations."

Shiro collapsed into one of the chairs by the desk. His mind whirled at the words. "What? I don't understand."

"You will preside over tonight's proceedings instead of the emperor."

"But how?"

"You are of the same build and height as the emperor. When you wear the imperial mask and robes, no one will question whether you are the emperor or not."

Shiro pictured himself negotiating with the Khaganate delegation and offending them by messing up a complex ritual. He would be responsible for plunging the empire back into the war. "I don't know how to preside over peace negotiations. I'm a simple clerk from the military supply division. I wouldn't know what to say."

"The emperor does not speak in public. Least of all to barbarians. You will sit and bless the negotiations with the presence of the emperor. We will teach you what you need to know."

"Is there no other way?" Shiro asked.

"No." Grandmaster Dalip got up and walked over to Shiro. "The barbarians need to see the emperor at the negotiations, otherwise they will take offence and break off the negotiations. So, we will give them the emperor they expect." Grandmaster Dalip placed a hand on Shiro's shoulder. "The empire needs you, Shiro."

"I will help in any way I can."

"Good. As a sign of the emperor's gratitude, he is promoting you to the internal affairs department. Your belongings will be moved tomorrow. For the rest of the day an aide will teach you what you need to know for the negotiations tonight. He's waiting outside." Grandmaster Dalip went back to sit behind the desk. He picked up a couple of the papers he had laid down when Shiro entered.

For a moment Shiro was unsure what to do. Grandmaster Dalip ignored him. He quietly got up and headed for the door.

"Shiro," Grandmaster Dalip's voice came from behind him as he reached the door. "Before you leave, let me stress that this is a very sensitive topic. The emperor would be very disappointed if anyone heard any rumors about his illness or your help. He would ensure that the source of the rumors or people close to the source would not be around to confirm them. I'm sure you understand."

Shiro gulped. "Yes, Grandmaster."

Grandmaster Dalip bent over his papers again. His posture made it clear the meeting was over. Shiro turned around and, with a feeling of trepidation, left as quietly as he could.

Negotiations

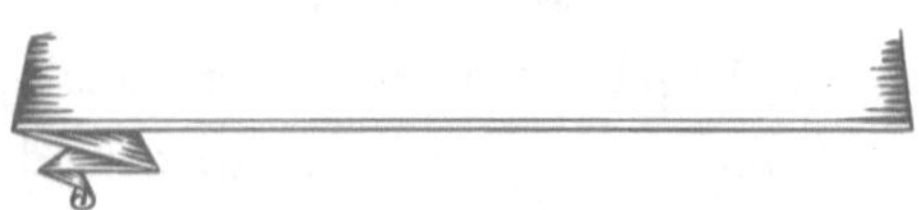

Shiro stood at the ready in front of the doors. He was sweating. The silken imperial robes felt unnatural against his skin. The gilded imperial mask, which made his shoulders and neck ache, made it difficult to breathe. How did the emperor wear this day in and day out? He wanted to hop from one foot to the next and scratch an itch on his left cheek. With difficulty, he kept his hands along his body as he had been instructed. The emperor does not fidget.

He focused on the little piece of woodworking of the door he could see through the narrow eye slits in the mask. The dark ebony was carved in swirls that together formed a demon in the center of the two doors. A golden sun shone behind it.

Finally, two servants pushed open the double doors. A herald announced him. "All hail Emperor Shozun Maharant the Third! Bow down and tremble for the conqueror of nations, the vanquisher of demons, and the bringer of dawn."

The throne room was laid out in a T shape, with the throne standing at the top of the T. The guests were divided into two groups, one on either side of the T. Furthest away from Shiro, on his left, was the delegation from the Khaganate. Closest to him, on his right, were the five ministers of state, with Grandmaster Dalip at their head.

Shiro walked into the room with slow strides after the herald had finished his proclamation. Everyone in the room lay on hands and knees, face pressed against the floor. The Jade Throne loomed at the front of the room. Shiro reached the raised dais. With exaggerated care he walked up the two steps and placed his hand on the armrest. A shiver ran up his arm when he touched the sacred throne. Finally, he turned and sat.

"You are in the presence of a God," the herald declared. "Rise now. Be honest and just, for you will be judged."

The crowd rose.

"I am Porga of Djura, emissary of the Khaganate," a man at the front of the Khaganite delegation said. "I speak for our exalted leader," He wore an exotic costume. A large turban in bright red and orange adorned his head. A moustache and pointed beard that ran to his navel framed a delicate mouth. A bright yellow-and-brown puffy shirt matched the turban. He gave a short bow from the middle. "I am honored by your reception and your presence. May our negotiations be fruitful."

Shiro gave a salute with his hand against his chest in welcome as he had been instructed. It was all the welcome he would give to the foreign barbarians. Speaking at these public meetings was beneath the emperor.

Grandmaster Dalip took up the sign. "Our emperor declares you our friend and guest, Porga. May our negotiations be fruitful indeed."

This was the sign for the Ministers and the members of the Khaganite delegation to mingle. It all looked very chaotic to Shiro. Delegates would meet in small groups of two or three people. They would talk for some time, walking around the room, and then drift apart again to form other groups. Most of the discussions took place too far away to overhear what was being said. But he caught drifts of conversations that were held close by.

"We want trade rights to be part of the treaty," a member of the Khaganate said.

"We can work with that," Master Jin answered. "We will lower the import taxes on grain and increase the export of our plum wine."

"We want to trade in iron and jade as well."

"That will be more difficult to arrange," Master Jin said. "Let me see what I can do." With that, the two of them drifted apart to record and discuss the different demands.

Shiro's mind started drifting. In his mind he saw a city besieged. An army of demons was camping outside the walls. Flames raged unchecked in several buildings, and dark smoke was heavy on the air. A tall white figure stood glimmering on the battlements and looked out over the battlefield outside the city. Around the man the defenders of the city rallied. They sallied forth from the gates of the city into the enormous mass of demons swirling outside.

A voice spoke inside Shiro's mind. *So it has been before, and so it will be again.* The voice sounded hollow, echoing through Shiro's head. Goose-bumps stood up on his arms.

"That is unacceptable." Grandmaster Dalip's voice dragged Shiro back to the present. Grandmaster Dalip was standing close by facing the emissary Porga. "We will not cede any lands as tribute in a peace treaty."

Shiro looked round. Everyone was focused on Grandmaster Dalip and the head of the Khaganite delegation. No one gave any indication they had heard the voice speaking. Perhaps he had simply dozed off. But the vision had felt different from a dream. Maybe the throne granted the emperor visions of far off places to aid him in his divine work.

"Those are our terms," Porga said. "We demand the western half of the Kaishing province up to the river Dainur. They will become a protectorate of the Khaganate as insurance for your adherence to the treaty. If there is no breach of contract for the next one hundred years, then the protectorate will be returned to you."

"They are the children of our heavenly emperor." Dalip raised his hand high. "We will not allow them to be ruled by barbarians. Not for one hundred years, not for a day."

"Those are our terms. We need insurance against the breach of contract."

"No."

"Then we are done here." He turned around, waved to his companions, and walked toward the exit. At the door he turned toward Dalip once more. "We will remain here in the city for the rest of the week should you change your mind." Porga then walked out of the door without a glance back.

Shiro watched the Khaganite delegation recede. Grandmaster Dalip had been right to refuse Porga's demand. It was unheard of to let barbarians rule over citizens of the empire, even if it was only for a hundred years. Shiro was confident that Grandmaster Dalip would find a way to appease the Khaganites and negotiate a treaty, without sacrificing any citizens of the empire.

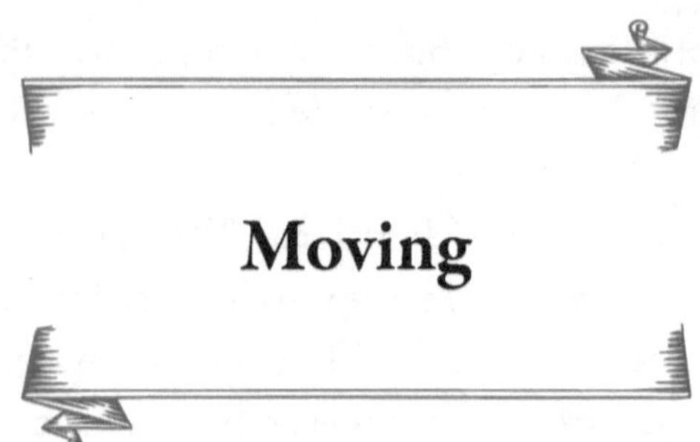

Moving

"You're really moving then," Taizo said.

"Yes," Shiro answered. They were sitting on a bench outside the living quarters of the trade clerks. The early afternoon sun gave off a pleasant warmth in the early spring. The first blossoms were appearing on the cherry trees lining the walkways. "It's part of the promotion to the internal affairs department." Shiro was giving the rehearsed speech about his move. "We need to be close to the ministers in case they have urgent tasks that need to be taken care of. Which is why I'm moving there. They were impressed by the speed of my work."

Taizo ran a hand through his sleek black hair. "Congratulations, I think." Taizo looked much the same as he had when the two of them had arrived in the Forbidden City together. He was half a hand taller than Shiro and sinuous. A thoughtful look on his angular face had replaced his usually boyish grin.

"Yeah, it's a big step. Two of the current five ministers of state came from the internal affairs department, as well as a handful of the departmental heads. The whole department is so close to the emperor."

"Do you think you'll ever meet him?" Taizo asked.

"The emperor?"

"Yeah."

Shiro rubbed his head and thought back to the meeting last night where he had worn the imperial regalia. "Maybe. They say the department is there to fulfill his personal wishes."

"Imagine the day when a simple provincial like you stands in the presence of the Bringer of Dawn. Who'd have guessed you'd get that far?"

"Simple provincial?" Shiro gave Taizo a shove against his shoulder. "You're even simpler than me. At least my parents are honest merchants. Everyone knows they stand way above simple fishermen." He gave out a laugh.

"You're still from the same backwater hole in the province as me, Shiro-don't you forget it." Taizo laughed as well.

"You're right. We've both gotten pretty far." Shiro looked at the sun, guessing the time. "We probably should get moving. I don't want to be late on my first day."

They jumped off the bench. Each grabbed a side of Shiro's trunk, and they set off through the Forbidden City. The dShirog sound of the new clerks learning the basics of imperial legislation by rote drifted through the open windows of the Hall of Grand Secretary. The air felt oppressed in the narrow streets they used to avoid the press of people which usually walked the broader avenues. The trade clerks lived close to the outer walls, near the Gate of the Eastern Lotus, while the living quarters for the internal affairs staff sat over the Gate of Imperial Benevolence, behind the Imperial Quarter.

The Gate of Imperial Benevolence sat in the old wall of the Forbidden City. Since the building of the gate, the Forbidden City had grown and now the gate only had a ceremonial function by distancing the students in the Palace of Literary Glory in the new part of the Forbidden City from the emperor who resided in the heart of the old city. The building itself rose for three stories above the streets. The original structure of the gate could still be seen in its ground floor, with thick walls and narrow windows. The upper two floors were a paneled wooden structure that had been added at a later date. The green-and-orange glazed roof was adorned with stone snakes crawling along the edges and top.

The bottom floor was given to the mess hall and the clerks' offices. The living quarters were at the top floor. They made for the stairs inside the arched gateway.

"Halt," a guard stepped out of a niche in the tunnel. "Where do you think you are going?"

"Hi! I'm Shiro. I was told to move my things here and report to Master Jin. He's expecting me this afternoon."

"Yes, you're expected." The guard pointed at Taizo. "Who's he?"

"Hi, I'm Taizo. Shiro's friend. Don't mind me."

"I do mind you. Authorized personnel only."

"I'm just helping him move. I'll be out of here before you know it."

The guard took a step forward and stuck out his halberd in front of them. "You're not allowed in."

Shiro placed a hand on Taizo's arm. "It's fine. I can take my stuff the rest of the way. It's not worth making a fuss over. Thanks for the help."

"I guess you're right. You'll have to tell me all about it later."

"Definitely. See you soon." Shiro waved to Taizo and dragged his trunk to the stairs.

On the third-floor landing he found Master Jin waiting for him, reading through some papers. The master's short hair was greying at the temples, but his athletic build belied his age. His outfit was less lavish than any Shiro had seen on other masters around the Forbidden City.

Master Jin got up as Shiro approached. He flowed gracefully from the bench. "There you are," he said. "You have the last room on the left. It just became available, so you might have some cleaning left to do. You'll meet Ray in a bit-he's discussing his trip with Master Joao. The others are out for the moment. Go put away your things and then come see me."

His room was spartan. The bed in the corner and a small table were the main furniture pieces. A wardrobe with an elaborate woodcarving on the door stood in one corner. Still, it was better than his room in the trade department, which he had shared with two other guys.

He dragged his trunk into the room. As he opened the wardrobe to unpack, he saw a small box discarded on the bottom shelf. A small painting lay next to it, depicting a lovely young girl with long black hair around a petit face. Her green eyes were vibrant, even in the gloom of the room. The box contained a stack of letters and an engagement bracelet. Strange that someone would leave this behind. He picked it up, determined to ask Master Jin how he could return it to its owner.

After dropping off his belongings, he went to find Master Jin in his office on the second floor. The room was light and airy, with a large window that overlooked the imperial gardens. A desk stood centrally in the room with chairs arranged around it.

"It's great to have you here, Shiro," Master Jin said. "I've heard good things about you."

"Thank you, Master."

"You've caught us at a bad time. Most people are out, but you'll meet them eventually, I'm sure. For now, Ray can mentor you."

"Yes, Master. Excuse me, but what exactly does the department of internal affairs do?"

Master Jin laughed. "That's a direct and interesting question, son. We do what the emperor asks of us. Which can be all sorts of jobs. In fact, I have one such job lined up for you. I'm sure you're aware that we have a delegation from the Khaganate visiting the Forbidden City."

Shiro nodded. "Yes, Master."

"Well, the emperor dearly wants to know how the balance of power inside the delegation lies."

Shiro scratched his head. "The balance of power, sir?"

"Yes. Who is friends with whom. Does Emissary Porga hold all the power, or are there multiple people who contribute ideas? That sort of thing."

"I understand."

"So, tonight, you and Ray will help serve the Khaganate delegation. Together you will spy on them and learn as much about them as possible. Even the smallest detail can get us on top in the upcoming negotiations."

"Tonight sir?" Shiro asked. His heart sped up as he pictured the foreign-looking delegation he had seen yesterday.

"Yes, just follow Ray's lead and you'll be fine. Go find him and tell him I sent you. He'll explain a few things." Master Jin got out the documents he was reading earlier again. With a gesture he made it clear the meeting was over. "That'll be all."

Shiro got up to leave. Then he remembered the painting he had taken.

"Master?"

Master Jin looked up, distracted.

"Where is the person who had my room before me?"

"He left. Why?"

Shiro took out the picture. "I've found this, and I thought he might like it back."

"Unfortunately, I don't have any way of reaching him. Feel free to do with it as you please. Anything else?"

"No, Master." Shiro walked out. Thoughts tumbled through his head as he went in search of Ray. If these were the sorts of jobs the internal affairs department performed for the emperor then it was no surprise the department was such a mystery. Working in the department clearly had downsides as well. He wondered if he would be able to do everything his emperor demanded of him.

Spying

Shiro walked through the embassy after Ray. He carried a platter of food while Ray held several jugs of wine. Ray turned out to be a jovial young man who didn't seem to have a worry in the world. He had been part of the internal affairs department for two years now. But other than that, he had said very little about what kind of work he had done in the department.

Shiro's instructions had been brief. Ray had given him a short run-down of the different members of the Khaganate delegation. The plan was simple. They would walk in with the food deliveries. They would leave the group and find a way to pose as servants during the course of the evening.

Their mission was to learn what the plans of the Khaganate delegation were. This would be crucial in the upcoming negotiations, Ray had told him. The Khaganites kept changing and increasing their demands. If Grandmaster Dalip didn't know what the Khaganites were after and what they were willing to accept at a minimum, then negotiating the peace treaty would be close to impossible without giving in to all the Khaganite demands. Grandmaster Dalip needed an edge.

Ray had smiled when Shiro had asked how they hoped to achieve this. Once inside they would ensure that the wine flowed abundantly. Wine loosened all tongues, and a drunk never noticed the servants, Ray had told him. They would listen in on the different conversations throughout the evening and keep note of who was friendly with whom. If this wasn't enough then they would search the embassy for the information Grandmaster Dalip needed.

The members of the delegation lounged on large sofas spread around the dining room. Servants carried steaming platters filled with roast chicken and veal or heaped high with steaming vegetables. Shiro and Ray made a tour around the room. Shiro offered everyone a chicken leg, while Ray topped up everyone's goblet while remarking that the wine matched the chicken perfectly.

Porga lay at the far end of the room. A belly dancer in yellow and purple silk jingled as she danced around him. He looked out over the room, casually chewing on a chicken leg. Ray went to top up his goblet. Porga waved his hand over his goblet, indicating he had enough for now.

Ray joined Shiro near the door leading to the kitchen. "Tonight may turn out to be a bit more complicated than we thought," Ray whispered. "They're not drinking nearly as much as I assumed they would. This could end up being a boring party."

Shiro's heart sank. This was his first real job for the ministry and at this rate it would be a disaster. "What do we do?" Master Jin hadn't looked like the kind of man who tolerated failure. Maybe he would even send Shiro back to the trade department.

"Do you think they'll notice if we just pour alcohol down their throat?" Ray gave a chuckle at his own joke.

"That's an idea."

"It was a joke, Shiro."

"I know." Shiro motioned for Ray to follow him. "Come with me. I saw something that might help." He headed into the kitchen. Ray shrugged and headed after him.

Shiro walked through the kitchen and past a couple of steaming pans. Two cooks stood near the hearth, arguing over the seasoning of the dessert. The smell of cinnamon and cardamom hung heavy in the air. Shiro walked straight to the pantry on the other side of the kitchen. Once inside, he closed the door behind him and Ray. "Look." He pointed to the top shelf.

"There's more bottles of booze. What about it?"

"If the Khaganites don't drink a lot, then our only option is to make them drink stronger stuff."

Ray shook his head. "You think they won't notice that they're drinking baiju instead of wine?"

"Of course they will." Shiro grabbed a couple of bottles from the shelves. "But they won't if we mix the baiju with wine and add in some spices. We'll call it a chef's special or something fancy like that."

Ray hesitated and rubbed his chin. "That might just work. Let's give it a try."

They grabbed several bottles of baiju and wine from the shelves. Shiro got a large pan from the kitchen, and they got to mixing the two drinks together. Ray went through the cupboards of the pantry until he had located the spices. "How much should I put in?" he asked.

"Just throw a whole bunch in and then give it a taste."

Ray put several spoonfuls of the different spices into the wine and stirred. He tried some with his spoon. "That's not bad, actually. And you don't even notice the alcohol much."

"Time to start serving, then," Shiro said.

They poured drinks and carried them to the eating Khaganites.

"What's this?" asked the first guest they served it to. He had a deep voice that matched his muscular frame and dark beard.

"Just a little drink the cook has put together before dessert." Ray managed to keep a straight face as he said it.

The man took a suspicious sip of the drink. His eyebrows rose and he smacked his lips. He thumped his companion sitting across from him on the arm. "Try this." He grabbed a goblet from Ray's tray and held it in front of his friend. His companion took the glass and tasted it with approval.

After these first two, serving the drinks went easier. Most of the Khaganites liked the drink and it went down easy. However, when Ray again offered Porga a drink the man refused again. "I have drunk enough for tonight," he said.

By the time the dessert was served, most Khaganites were happily inebriated. Shiro stood close to the wall, arms behind his back, eavesdropping on a group of delegates.

"I don't like this place," a man wearing a brown shirt and a white silk shawl said. "There's too much rain. I miss the desert air."

His companion, in a dark green outfit, grunted in assent. "I hear you Maruf. The food's all wrong too. Too much heat in it. It's like they're trying to compensate for the cold weather."

"What are we even doing here, negotiating?" Maruf said. "Porga just keeps demanding more and more."

"Dunno. Maybe he just benefits more from a war or he has some plan to outplay the Khan."

"I don't like it one bit. They're proud people here. If he pushes too hard, they might just forget we're emissaries."

"You worry too much, Maruf. We'll be fine. And look on the bright side, they do have beautiful women here."

"Indeed. Remember those from three nights ago? They were pretty wild."

Shiro shifted his attention as the conversation drifted over all the women they had met over the years. Ray, who was standing on the other side of the room signaled for him to come over. Shiro took on what he hoped was a casual posture and strolled along the wall towards Ray.

"Have you learned anything useful?" Ray asked.

"A couple are wondering about Porga's commitment to actually reaching a deal," Shiro said. "Most just want to get out of here as soon as possible. Also, it seems like there's two camps in the delegation. One loyal to Porga and one who follows Maruf."

"I noticed the same thing. It seems like Porga has his own agenda next to the official one from the Khan and not too many friends in his own delegation."

"What's next?" Shiro asked.

"I think we have learned all we can for tonight," Ray said. "There's just a couple of things left to do before we can escape. Can you create a distraction?"

"A distraction, why?"

"I don't have time to explain everything. But I just need to ensure that everyone's attention is focused elsewhere for a while. Give me a count of two hundred and then start." Ray walked off.

Shiro started counting in his head and looked around him. He thought hard about what he could use for a distraction. Nothing obvious came to mind. He would be spotted the instant he tried something. He walked out of the room as his count reached fifty and started down the corridor. There was nothing useful there. One hundred. He tried a side door. It opened into a study, illuminated by a couple of candles. Bookshelves lined the walls and high-backed chairs stood around the fireplace. A desk littered with papers stood against the near wall. On it, a bust of the Khan had been used as a paperweight. Nothing here was going to help him.

"Can I help you, sir?" a voice came from behind.

Shiro jumped. He turned around and saw a servant standing in the door opening. "Sorry, you surprised me," Shiro said. "I, uhm," Shiro searched his mind for something to say. "I was looking for the restroom."

"You just missed it, sir. Down the hallway, next door on the right."

A thought occurred to Shiro. "Thank you. After you, good sir." He motioned the servant to lead the way. He followed the servant. When he passed the desk, he grabbed the bust of the Khan. With two quick steps he caught up with the servant. He swung the bust high and hit him on the back of the head. The servant drifted to the floor like a leaf from a tree.

Shiro stared at the man and then at the bust in his hand. He dropped it. It clattered on the ground next to the servant.

"I'm sorry," he mumbled. He wondered if he had killed the servant. Surely he hadn't hit him that hard.

Two hundred. The distraction! He sprinted down the hallway, back to the dining room. He threw open the door as hard as he could. It slammed against the wall. He ran in shouting. "Murder! Murder!"

Everyone in the room jumped up. Several Khaganites drew their weapons. Shiro ran further into the room, pointing down the hall. "There's a dead body there! Thieves! Murder!"

One of the Khaganites grabbed his arm. "What's going on? He asked.

Shiro looked at the Khaganite with wide open eyes. He took a deep breath and pretended to calm himself. "There is a body lying in the hallway. Back by the study. Someone killed a servant. Down the hall, quick." Shiro waved with his arms towards the door. "Maybe the murderer is still around."

The Khaganites jumped up and ran down the hallway. Shiro found himself alone in the room. "Best not stick around, I guess," he said to himself under his breath. He ran towards the kitchen on the other side of the room. There, he forced himself to walk calmly past the cooks to the servant's entrance.

The chilly night air flowed over Shiro as he stepped outside. He released a breath he hadn't realized he was holding. Maybe tonight would be a success after all. Ray at least had seemed confident they had learned enough. He looked to see if Ray was around, but he was nowhere in sight. Ray could take care of himself.

Shiro set off towards the gates of the embassy complex. A guard was sitting next to the exit. "What's happening?" the guard asked. "I thought I heard some shouting inside."

"I'm not sure," Shiro answered. "A wild party I guess. Like the one they had a couple of nights ago."

"You're probably right."

Shiro walked through the gate. "Good night," he waved to the guard, who grunted in assent. He walked towards the street corner, expecting a shout for him to stop. Nothing happened as he rounded the corner and got out of sight. When no one could see him, he started running through the Forbidden City, back to his room.

He only slowed when the department of internal affairs building rose up ahead. The feeling of dread that one of the Khaganites would come after him finally fell off his shoulders.

"You took your time," Ray's voice came out of the shadows at the foot of the building. "Your distraction was a bit overly dramatic perhaps, but it got the job done. Not bad for a first night out."

"Why did you need one?"

"I had to poison Porga," Ray stated matter of factly.

"What?"

"Shhh." Ray motioned with his hands. "Do you want everyone to hear?"

"Is he," Shiro hesitated. "Is he dead?"

"No, he'll live. Probably," the last was added as an afterthought. "He should just be tied to his toilet for the next week or two."

"But why?"

Ray shrugged. "I don't know. Dalip wanted it done. I don't ask too many questions. If you want my guess, it's probably something to do with the negotiations."

"That is horrible."

"They're the enemy. They threaten our way of life. Anything's fair in war."

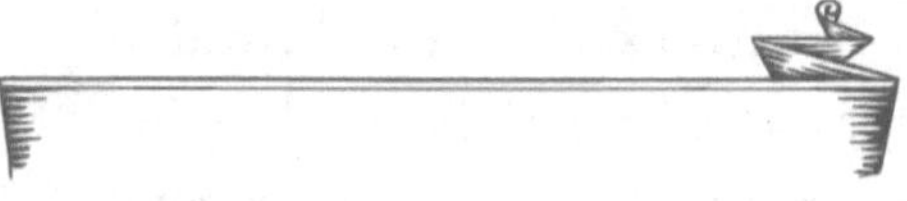

Emperor again

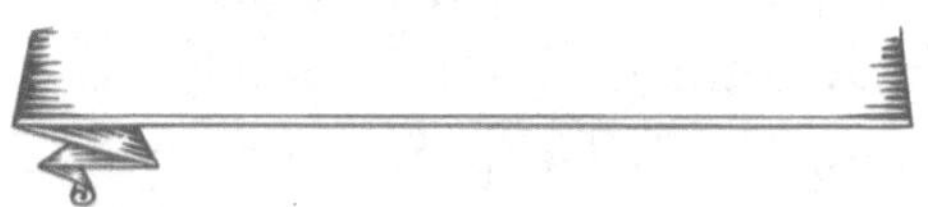

Shiro strode to the throne, masked and dressed in the embroidered imperial robes once more. Today he wore a yellow silk robe with a green pattern highlighting the central trim. Over the past two days he had kept looking over his shoulders, worried that a Khaganite would search him out and drag him back to the embassy. But nothing had happened. The sun had risen as it always had and the Khaganites had raised no fuss. And then this morning Grandmaster Dalip had informed him that the emperor was still ill and that he needed Shiro to preside over another round of negotiations.

Shiro sat on the Jade Throne. "You are in the presence of a God," the herald declared. "Rise now. Be honest and just, for you will be judged."

People around the room rose to their feet. Shiro had to squint against the sun coming through the skylight overhead. One of the men from the embassy, Maruf, strode forward. "I am Maruf, emissary of the Khaganate," he said. "I speak for our exalted leader, the Khan of Khans. I regret to inform you that Porga has fallen ill. It now falls to my humble self to lead the negotiations."

Grandmaster Dalip bowed to Maruf. "I am sorry to hear that. I hope it's nothing serious."

"Our physicians ensure me that he will fully recover in due course. But for the moment he's unable to leave his bed."

"The emperor will pray for his recovery," Grandmaster Dalip said with a flourish towards Shiro. "I heard you also had a break-in a couple of nights ago. I have asked my guards to investigate. I hope nothing of value went missing."

"No indeed, Master Dalip. Someone attacked one of our servants. But he was spotted and had to flee before he could steal anything."

"I'm glad to hear," Grandmaster Dalip said. "Have you given our negotiations some more thought? We can't match the demands you made last time. But we can work out some very favorable trade deals for you. And of course, we will also compensate you and your delegation for the time spent on this extra round of negotiations."

Maruf smiled and nodded. "I think we can come to an understanding. My friend Farooq here," he pointed at a short, stocky man behind him, "he knows all about trade agreements. I'm sure he can work with your people on something. Then you and I have some time to discuss the other parts of the treaty."

The groups in front of the throne mingled. Master Chin walked over to Farooq, obviously intent on getting a good trade agreement. Maruf and Grandmaster Dalip wandered off to one side of the reception room. Curious, Shiro strained his ears to overhear what they were discussing.

Grandmaster Dalip was talking. "I think we can make a treaty very favorable for everyone involved. Our emperor would be very thankful to the people instrumental to getting a good deal."

Maruf nodded. "A prolonged war is never good for any of the involved countries. I prefer peace and mutual respect so all parties involved can trade and prosper. I believe we can make this happen now that Porga is unavailable."

"Yes, it's a shame that he would become ill at such a crucial time. I pray that he recovers swiftly."

"Indeed, though not too swiftly." Maruf chuckled.

"The emperor is very grateful to you personally for keeping the talks moving. He would like to know how he can thank you."

The two men walked out of earshot of Shiro.

As Shiro's attention wandered, his vision shifted. The Forbidden City spread out below him, like a bird would see it. Everything was dark, except for the Imperial Quarter, which sat illuminated in the middle of the city. Shadows moved through the streets, insignificant compared to the majesty of the emperor.

As the vision faded to black, the voice Shiro had heard last time spoke. *You're back.* It was a statement. *You're not a ruler.* Shiro could only nod in answer. *This is beyond you.*

The throne room came back in focus. Shaken, Shiro tried to pay attention to the proceedings going on in front of him. What had the voice meant? Of course he wasn't the emperor. Maybe the emperor always got these visions and knew what they meant. He was the divine Bringer of Dawn after all. It made sense that his holiness received divine inspiration at times.

TWO HOURS LATER SHIRO was back at the interior affairs building. He sat on a landing on the top floor and looked out over the Forbidden City. The negotiations had concluded swiftly. Some trade agreement had been drawn up. The empire and the Khaganate would exchange some princes to strengthen the bonds between the countries. And the empire would provide a shipment in rubies as payment to the Khaganate. Shiro had been surprised at how fast the deal had come together. He had expected the talks to last as long as the previous time.

Ray walked over. "You've got the evening off as well." It was a statement and not a question.

"Yeah, I finished early." Shiro had picked up the habit from the other clerks around the interior affairs building to be vague about the work he did.

"You want a drink?" Ray held out a cup.

"Sure."

They drank in silence for a while. Lights shone through windows across the Forbidden City below. It created an image as if they were looking down on the stars from far above.

Across the Forbidden City a fireworks rocket exploded, showering yellow and silver sparkles across the sky. Another rocket went up, this one red. The emperor really was going all out in an attempt to impress the Khaganate delegation and celebrate the successful conclusion of the negotiations. A third rocket contained a golden fountain raining down.

Ray nodded towards the fireworks display. "I once saw a fireworks storage room blow up in Chingao. The blast took out half a city block. I haven't been able to enjoy fireworks from up close since. They give me the shivers."

"Really?" Shiro couldn't picture Ray getting the shivers from anything.

"Yeah. I'm glad they keep the fireworks stored on the other side of the City underneath the Pavilion of Tranquility. I asked after I got back from Chingao. I couldn't sleep until I knew I was far enough away."

Shiro looked at Ray. He looked more approachable than any other time Shiro had known him. "Do you know what happened to the guy who used to live in my room?" Shiro asked.

"You mean Poshu?"

Shiro shrugged. "I guess."

"He just disappeared one day," Ray said.

"Where did he go?"

"Don't know. Why do you ask?"

"He left some stuff behind in the room. I thought maybe he'd want it back. Did he have any family maybe?"

"Not that I know of. He came from some backwater town in the province somewhere. I don't think his family could even point out the Forbidden City on a map."

"Do you know if he maybe had some friends in the city who would know?"

"You could check the merchant district. I think he used to visit some places there from time to time. Maybe someone there knows him."

It wasn't much of a lead, but at least it gave a starting point for Shiro's search. He placed a hand on Ray's shoulder. "Thanks. I'll check it out some day."

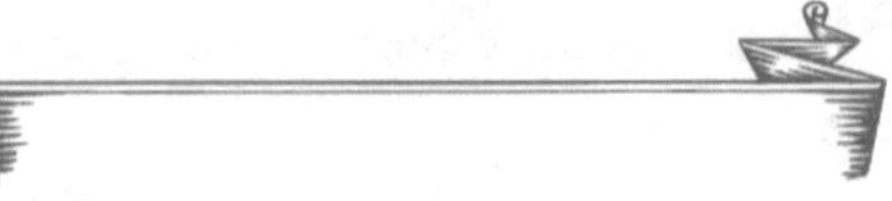

A night out

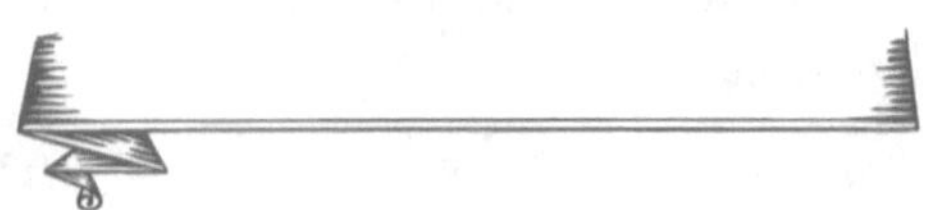

"So, explain to me again," Taizo said, "what are we doing here?" They were walking over the cobbled streets leading from the Forbidden City to Hinan's merchant district. The shops they passed were closing up for the night. A light drizzle muffled the sounds around them.

"Like I said," Shiro answered, "I felt like getting a drink somewhere."

"You never go for a drink. And why don't we just go to a bar near the Forbidden City?"

Shiro searched his mind for a good explanation. Taizo would call him crazy if he told him about the portrait. "Don't you want a change of scenery every now and then?" he said, trying to buy some time.

"I do, all the time. But," Taizo pointed a finger at Shiro, "you don't."

Shiro pulled Taizo to the side of the street. "If you really must know," Shiro dropped his voice. "I'm looking into something for the department of Internal Affairs. I can't talk about it much, but it means I've got to have a look around the district here."

"You mean we're spying on our own people here?" Taizo raised his eyebrows.

"No, of course not. It's nothing like that." They started moving again. "I just need some information."

"So, spying."

Shiro sighed. "Just please, don't tell anyone."

They passed a fur merchant who was just closing up. On the corner ahead lights shone out of the windows on the second story of the Traveling Head Inn. It was one of the central places in the merchant district. It stood on a busy crossing. The road ahead went over the Trinity Isle Bridge and from there on to the harbor.

"All right, I was just messing with you. I've got your back." Taizo stroked his chin. "Though I do wonder, since it's official business, will your department pay the bill for tonight."

Shiro gave him an incredulous look and Taizo started laughing. "Just kidding." Taizo thumped his shoulder. "I'll just let you pay."

They crossed the street to the inn. A burly doorman with a club hanging from his belt eyed them as they headed in. Their eyes needed a moment to adjust to the gloom inside. The heat from the blazing fire in the hearth was oppressive after the damp outside. Smells of grilled meat and stews wafted towards them. The bar was straight ahead across the room. Niches where people could conduct private business lined the walls. A staircase in the far corner led up to the second story.

"Why don't you find us a seat?" Shiro asked. "I'll get us something to drink." Shiro headed over to the bar.

The bartender had a spiky moustache in the middle of his bald, round head. He gave a nod at Shiro "What do you want?"

"Two beers please." Shiro got out a stack of coins and played with them a bit.

The bartender grabbed two mugs and wiped a cloth through them. Shiro wasn't sure the cloth actually made them any cleaner. Shiro took the painting of the girl out of his pocket as the bartender put the beers in front of him. "Do you know this girl?" he asked.

The bartender hardly glanced at the picture. "Nope. Never seen her."

Shiro pushed the stack of coins forward. "For the beers. And maybe it'll help your memory."

"Let me see that again," the bartender said. He bent forward to take a closer look at the picture. "Yeah, my memory suddenly got better." He grabbed the pile of coins. "She used to come here sometimes. Haven't seen her in a while. I think she lives somewhere around porter alley. Maybe ask around there."

Shiro put the picture away and grabbed the beers. "Thanks."

Taizo had found a spot in the corner near the hearth. Shiro weaved towards him. "There you go." He put the mugs down.

"What do we do now?" Taizo asked.

"Nothing special. Just listen a bit if you hear something interesting. We'll stay here for a drink and then move on."

Shiro leaned back and nursed his drink. He let his attention drift from one conversation around him to the next. To his left, a couple of men were discussing the problems they were having with the weather. The rain of the past weeks had ruined a lot of crops, raising prices across the empire.

Another group was discussing the trade agreement between the empire and the Khaganate. And to his right a man was complaining about how his niece had just run off. She had probably eloped with some poor shmuck.

Taizo said something which pulled him back. "Sorry, what did you say?"

"I was just thinking that it felt like a boring party here. It's too quiet or something."

Shiro looked around and saw Taizo was right. It was quiet for dinner time. The groups of people were mainly sticking to themselves, talking in hushed tones.

"You're right. Let's finish our drink and go somewhere else."

They drank up in silence. When they got outside again, night had fallen. Most people had fled inside to escape from the drizzle, leaving the streets empty. They stuck up their hoods, drew their cloaks around them and headed deeper into the merchant district.

Porter alley ran between the main canal and the central market. In the early morning it was busy with porters moving goods from the canal to the market. At this time of night, the only people around were visiting one of the two inns in the alley. They decided to go to the Porter's Lounge, which lay closest to the market square.

The Porter's Lounge was bright compared to the Traveling Head. A large chandelier full of candles hung from the ceiling. It had a small common room with maybe twenty guests in total. A bar was tucked in the corner to the left of the door. Stairs leading up to the second floor were on the right, a set of doors leading to the kitchen underneath them.

Shiro threw back his hood and shook off the worst of the rain. He looked out over the room for an empty spot. A serving girl from the kitchen walked in, bearing a tray covered in steaming plates, which brought with them the smells of cloves

and nutmeg. Shiro sucked in his breath. The girl's green, slant-
ed eyes stood out, even from across the room. She was the girl
from the picture.

He pointed to an empty table in the corner. "We can sit
there. Shall we get some food as well? All the walking has made
me hungry."

Taizo raised an eyebrow. "Sure. If you get us another beer
to go with it, I'm game."

They sat and Taizo waved to the serving girl. With Taizo
looking the other way, Shiro casually laid her picture on the
corner of the table.

After serving several tables the girl arrived at their table.
Her black hair was tied back, making her face appear thinner
than in the picture. "Good evening gentlemen," she said.
"What," her eye fell on her picture lying next to Shiro and she
stumbled on the sentence. "I, uhm," she drew in a breath. "I
mean, can I get you something to drink? And perhaps some
food on the side?"

"Two beers," Taizo said.

"And two plates of food. The stew smells great," Shiro
added.

"Of course, sirs." She walked off again.

"Cute girl," Taizo said. "She's got a nice swing to her hips."

"You only think of one thing." Shiro shook his head. "But
she has a cute face indeed." He pocketed the picture again before Taizo could notice it.

Their conversation drifted over the different girls they had
met over the years. After a while, the bartender brought them
two steaming plates of food.

"Not bad at all for pub grub," Taizo said. "Another reason to come back here, besides the serving girl."

"Indeed it is," Shiro answered. "Speaking of which, I haven't seen her in a while. Where did she go?"

"I dunno."

"You want another drink?" Shiro asked. When Taizo nodded, Shiro walked over to the bar and waved at the bartender that he wanted two beers. The bartender nodded and a short while later came over with two large mugs of beer.

"Thanks," Shiro said. "You look pretty busy here all by yourself."

"It's a decent night," he answered. "Better than many have been in the past couple of weeks. People have been hesitant to go out at night lately."

"Really?"

"Yeah, too many muggings from what I hear."

"What happened to the girl who took our order?" Shiro asked.

"Lyn? She wasn't feeling too well. So, I sent her home."

"Sorry to hear that. I've got some stuff that belongs to her. Do you know where I can find her?"

"I think she's got a place over near the fish market." The bartender waved to the back of the inn. "An apartment in one of the side streets I think."

"Thanks." Shiro took up the beers and walked back to Taizo.

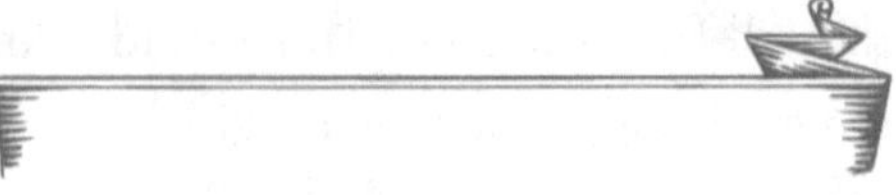

Falling out

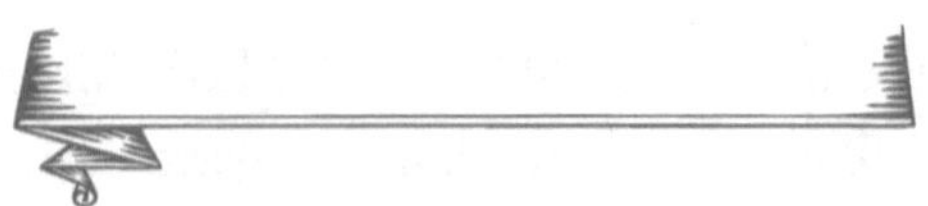

Shiro and Taizo were walking back towards the Forbidden City in silence. They had drunk a couple more beers in the Porter's Lounge and enjoyed the food. They had listened to the stories floating around them and reminisced on everything they had been through. The moon was already sinking to the horizon by the time the Forbidden City came in view again.

Taizo turned to Shiro. "Who are we now going to report to?"

Shiro shook himself out of a reverie. "Sorry? What do you mean, report?"

"You know, your mission for the Ministry of Internal Affairs. We spent all night spying, didn't we? We need to inform your superior about everything we learned, don't we?"

"Ah, is that what you mean. Look, I told you, we weren't spying."

Taizo sarcastically held up his hands in apology. "Right, sorry. We were just gathering information without telling anyone who we were. You'll still inform someone about that information."

Shiro searched for an answer. "I'll just write a report or something in the morning."

They started walking again. Shiro wondered about the best way to continue searching for this girl, Lyn the bartender had called her.

"You'll mention my help, right?" Taizo asked. "In the report I mean."

"Sure, sure."

"I know that tone." Taizo grabbed Shiro's arm. "You're not even listening, are you?"

"I'm sorry. My mind was just preoccupied."

"Look, this is important to me. A good word about me in a report will be good for my career."

"Yes, I'll mention how helpful you've been tonight." Shiro had a vision about Taizo bragging to Master Chin about being in some made up report. He needed to stop that from happening. "But you must know that most reports in the ministry are classified. You can't actually mention this to anyone. They will either not know what you're talking about or pretend not to know."

"I can't imagine a report about two guys having a drink being classified."

"I'm sorry Taizo."

"Like hell you are." Taizo made a dismissive gesture with his arm. "It's very convenient for you. We work on this together and you get all the credits."

"No, it's not like that at all. I just don't want you to be disappointed."

"That's easy for you to say, mister I'm so perfect I get invited into the Ministry of Internal Affairs!" Taizo shouted. "You know, some people actually have to do real work to just keep their job.'"

"Calm down, please." Shiro made a shushing motion with his hands. "You drank too much to be having this discussion."

"Bah, I am calm! I thought we were friends. And do you know what friends do?" Taizo paused a second as if waiting for an answer. "They help each other. You? You just freewheel through life and get lucky break after lucky break. I've supported you every step of the way. And now I ask for one simple favor and you just dismiss it?"

"Look, I already said I would mention your help."

"In the mysterious report I can never see or mention to anyone else."

"I'm sorry Taizo."

Taizo made a dismissive gesture. "No, you're not." He turned away from Shiro and walked away. "Thanks for nothing."

"Taizo, wait."

"Goodbye Shiro. Good luck with your new friends." Taizo looked over his shoulder. "Next time you need help, ask them instead." He walked off without looking back, leaving Shiro standing in the middle of the road.

Searching for Lyn

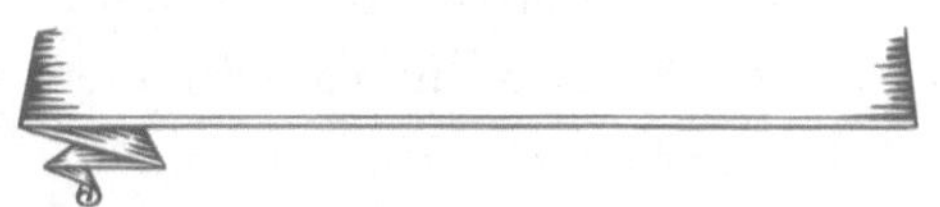

Shiro walked through Hinan towards the fish market. Grey clouds floated overhead, but it looked like it would stay dry for now. On a few rare occasions the morning sun had even peeked through the clouds. He hadn't spoken to Taizo again after their argument two days ago. The one time he'd seen Taizo, Taizo had simply ignored him and walked the other way. And since Shiro hadn't wanted to bring anyone from the ministry of Internal affairs with him, he was all by himself.

Two carts passed him as he entered the fish market. In several places around the market alleys led into the gloom between the houses. A group of beggars sat on the corner, holding up their hands to any passer-by. They had not been here last time Shiro had been to a market in the city. Fish mongers cried out to promote their wares. The smallest stalls, which were little more than a board on trestles, had trout or catfish on display. The bigger stalls had both and some crabs or crayfish. The smell of fish overpowered all the other scents of the city.

How would he ever find Lyn in this chaos? Looking for someone here was like looking for a Kaisho stone in a bowl. There were too many streets to search through. And even if he could, there was no guarantee that Lyn would be home or that he would see her. He made a tour of the market, hoping inspiration would strike. Nothing occurred to him. He sighed and picked an alley at random.

The alley was even gloomier than the market had been. When he stretched his arms he touched the houses on both sides at the same time. A heap of refuse lay against a wall on the cobblestones and the smell of human excrement warred with the smell of fish for attention. This was not the sort of place where a woman would live by herself. He turned back to the market, determined to look in on another side street of the market.

As he turned he saw a kid sitting on the ground with his back against the first house in the alley. The kid wore rags. His arms were like twigs, greasy hair was plastered to his face with streaks of dirt. "You've got a coin to spare, sir? Or maybe some bread?" The kid asked when he noticed Shiro looking.

Shiro was struck with an idea. He fished a small coin out of his pocket and threw it to the kid. "There you go. And I've got another one if you help me." He got the little painting of Lyn out of his pocket. "I'm looking for this lady. Have you seen her?"

The kid gave the picture a look, tilting his head sideways, first one way and then another. "Nope, sir."

Shiro tossed the kid the second coin. "If you find her for me, you'll get another one. She's said to live somewhere around the fish market. Just make sure she doesn't see you. I will be in the North-West corner of the market if you find her."

"I'll definitely find her for you." The kid got up and ran off.

Back in the market, Shiro did the same thing with several other beggars. None of them knew her, but five pairs of eyes who knew the way around here would see more than he could by himself. Shiro took up position in the north-west corner of the market.

He had just settled in to wait when the first kid he'd approached came walking across the market. "I found her for ye," he said. "She lives in one of the alleys that way," the kid waved vaguely across the marketplace. "I'll take you. Show you were she lives. Come, come," the kid motioned for Shiro to follow and started back the way he'd come.

Shiro hurried after the kid with a skip in his step. That had gone a lot faster than expected. He had been sure he would have needed a couple of days to track her down.

On the other side of the fish market they dove into the warren of alleys. Shiro kept track of the twists and turns, but after two lefts, followed by a right, another left and a curve to the right he had lost all sense of direction. They could have been walking in circles for all he knew. It was certainly much further than he had expected.

At last they took a right turn and then the boy slowed down. The alley they were in had a dead-end, a wall two stories high blocking the far end. The brick houses on both sides had no windows looking into the alley.

"Which house is it?" Shiro asked his guide.

The boy turned towards him. "I'm sorry, sir."

"What do you mean?"

A voice came from behind them. "Good afternoon, sir. We noticed that your purse looked awfully heavy. So we would like to offer our services to help you carry it."

Shiro spun around. Three men blocked the entry to the alleyway. They carried heavy wooden clubs and their clothes were in much better repair than those of the kid which had taken Shiro here. The middle one, who had been talking, was taller than his two companions by a hand at least. When Shiro turned around this one held up his hand.

Shiro looked around for options. There was no escape at his back. The walls on all sides were at least two stories high. And fighting even just one of them would probably go badly. But he didn't want to give up his hard earned wages either. Shiro walked forward, acting as if he was searching for his purse. When he was just out of reach of the group, he threw a handful of small coins at the leader to distract him and ran for the gap on the leader's right.

Shiro closed the gap quickly, his fear lending him extra speed. He passed the leader in heartbeats. He would get away. Then something struck his leg. He stumbled and fell face first to the cobblestones. The thug on the right had reacted fast and had kicked Shiro's legs from under him.

The three thugs came in and kicked Shiro, who curled up into a ball, protecting his stomach and face. Shiro cried out with each kick, tears streaming down his face.

Finally they had enough. One of them searched through Shiro's pockets and grabbed his purse. Shiro heard the jingle of coins being distributed and feet walking away. He tasted blood in his mouth.

"I'm really sorry, sir," the voice of the beggar kid came from close by his ear. "But me family's got to eat. And with the city flooded with refugees from the war and all that, a boy's got to take what he can."

After that Shiro was alone. He lay on the ground, taking deep breaths until he stopped shuddering. The shadows had moved up the walls around him by the time he found the strength to move. He staggered upright and leaned against the wall to prevent him from falling over again.

When the world stopped spinning he groaned and pushed off the wall. The first thing he needed to do was find a way out of here. He had lost all sense of direction. Since this meant that all choices were equal, he picked a street at random and started walking.

He came to a corner and looked down both alleys. He picked the largest one, figuring it had the best chance of getting him out of this warren. The pain in his sides subsided a bit as he stumbled through the alleys.

The sun was setting by the time he staggered into a broader street. A cart passed him by and he could see more than ten paces ahead of him. The houses here had actual windows and a tree offered some shade in a little square. He had made his way out of the warren. There was a bakery straight across the street, a spice shop a bit further down the road, as was an inn called the Smelly Cat. It was the sort of street where a single, young lady would want to live.

He walked over to the inn. Despite its name it looked friendly enough and the smell of a fish stew coming out the door was wonderful. Shiro first headed over to the restroom where he washed the dirt from his hands and face. Back in the common room, he went to order a drink when he realized he had no money left. Instead he took out Lyn's picture and waited for the innkeeper to notice him.

"You look like shit," the innkeeper said by way of introduction when he came over. "What can I get you?"

"I got robbed on the way here," Shiro answered. "So I've got no money for anything. I just want some information." He placed the painting on the bar. "I'm looking for her. I've been told she lives around here somewhere."

"What do you need her for?"

"I've found some stuff that belongs to her. I would like to return it."

The innkeeper looked at the picture again. "Yeah, I know her. I once told her about a job as serving girl in an inn down in the city. She lives two streets over, in Nandarian road. It should be the fifth or sixth house on this side."

"Thanks." Shiro pocketed the picture and walked out.

Nandarian road looked similar to the road the Smelly Cat had been on. The houses were two or three stories tall, with many of them divided into apartments.

The ground floor apartment of the fifth house from the corner was completely dark. Next to it a staircase ran to a second floor apartment. Light shone through one of the windows upstairs. He headed up the stairs and knocked. Either Lyn lived there or it was one of her neighbors.

The scraping of a chair was followed by the steps of someone approaching. The door opened and light streamed out on to the top of the landing.

"You!" Lyn shouted. She slammed the door shut.

Shiro knocked again.

"Go away! I want nothing to do with you."

"Please. I only need a moment." Shiro said through the closed door.

"I know all about you guys. I don't want any business with the Ministry."

"I'm not here for the Ministry. I'm just looking for Poshu. I've got some of his stuff."

It went quiet inside. Shiro waited. "Are you still there?" He asked at last.

The door opened a bit again. Lyn looked through the crack. Her long hair framed her face and accented her cheekbones. She was even more striking than in the picture. "What did you say?" She asked.

Shiro took out Poshu's box and held it out to Lyn. "I found this in my room. I think Poshu forgot to take it when he moved."

Lyn grabbed the box. "Thank you," she said grudgingly. "But I still don't want anything to do with the Ministry. Goodnight." She closed the door again, leaving Shiro standing in the dark at the top of the stairs.

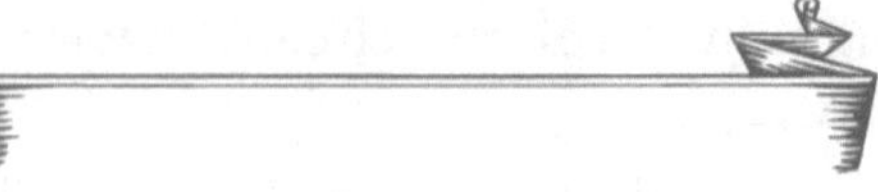

The other emperor

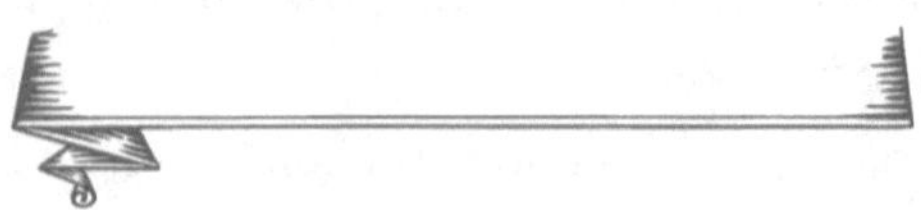

S hiro knocked on the door of Grandmaster Dalip's study. He stepped back and waited. As usual, the summons didn't contain any clue about why Grandmaster Dalip wanted to see him.

"Enter." Grandmaster Dalip's voice was curt and direct.

Shiro opened the door and headed in. Grandmaster Dalip sat bent over a pile of papers on his desk. Shiro crossed the carpet which covered most of the floor between the desk and the door. He stopped before the desk, waiting until Grandmaster Dalip would notice him, looking at his feet. The carpet depicted a demon cowering beneath the jade throne.

Grandmaster Dalip finished reading a document, set an signature at the bottom and looked up. "Welcome Shiro, how are you finding the Ministry of Internal Affairs?"

"It's great, sir." Shiro felt more was needed as an answer. "The work is varied and rewarding. It's everything I dreamed it would be."

"Good, good. I've heard some great things about you from Master Jin. It's nice to see that we made the right call with you."

"Thank you, sir" Shiro gave a short bow. That was amazing praise, coming from the grandmaster himself, though surely he hadn't been called here to be told this.

Grandmaster Dalip steepled his hands and looked directly at Shiro. "This is why we've decided to send you on a mission. It will be tough, but we think you're ready."

"I won't let you down, sir."

"I'm sure you won't." A small smile played over Grandmaster Dalip's lips.

"We have received news from Nan province. Some nobles have started a rebellion. They claim that a false emperor sits on the jade throne and that they have located the one true descendant of Emperor Jiu Qui. Their claim is of course preposterous." Shiro nodded in assent. "But," Grandmaster Dalip continued, "we need someone to investigate. We need to know which nobles support this false emperor and where this false emperor comes from. If we can find out what these people want, we can control them."

"Of course, sir" Shiro said.

"We need you to travel to Jaira in the Nan province and make contact with them. Negotiate and see if we have something we can offer them to make this go away."

"How can you be sure we have something they want?" Shiro asked.

"Everyone wants something." Dalip sounded certain. "It's usually money or power or both. If you know what someone wants then you can either give it to them to make them go away or make sure they see no way of getting it and make them give up."

Grandmaster Dalip took a small box from a drawer in his desk and put it in front of Shiro. "Take this with you. It contains enough money to get you to Nan province and back and a few other useful odds and ends. Make certain to also bring the box. We have some contacts throughout the empire. They will recognize the box and aid you if you need it."

Shiro picked up the box. It was a lot heavier than he had expected from the size of it. There must be a lot of coins in there indeed. It looked like a small treasure chest. The lid was inlaid with a jet-black stone in the shape of a five-pointed star.

"Thank you, sir."

"Master Jin will give you the details of your travel itinerary. Go see him."

"Yes, master." Shiro turned and walked towards the door.

"One more thing, Shiro." Shiro turned back around. "I've heard you're digging into Poshu's affairs. I must advise you to let that rest. He has left the ministry and that's that."

"Yes master."

Grandmaster Dalip waved his hand in dismissal.

Nan Province

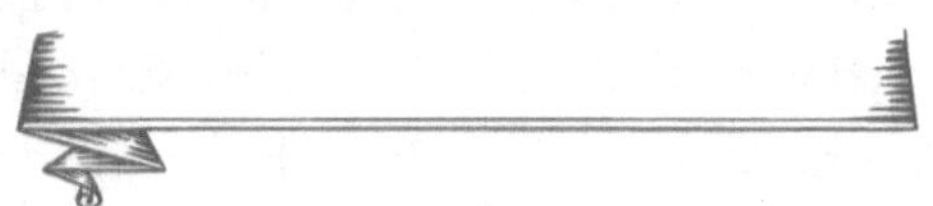

Shiro rode up the winding path towards the castle towering over Jaira. The sandstone of the fort colored a deep red in the setting sun. The imperial flag showing the dragon roaring at the sun flew above the gate. However, the imperial crest denoting the emperor was one unknown to Shiro. The iron gates, which were as thick as his upper arm, stood open, with a couple of helmeted guards in plate mail lounging outside them in the last rays of the sun. Shiro felt small as he craned his neck to see the top of the gatehouse.

Shiro dismounted and approached the guards. Their spears rested against the wall next to them. "Hail, I am Shiro of Liang." The guard on the left opened an eye to look at Shiro. "I have been sent by the Ministry of Internal Affairs." At this, both guards jumped erect. One of them grabbed his spear and aimed it at Shiro.

"What do you want?" the other guard asked.

"I have been sent to parlay with the Lords of Nan on behalf of the ministry. We wish to speak in an open manner to prevent any bloodshed."

"All right, we'll let them know you're here." The left guard nodded at his companion, who ran off into the fort. Shiro looked around while he waited. The walls of Jaira, in the valley far below the fort, were already cloaked in shadows. The rice paddies around the town looked like a patchwork blanket with the main road running through it like some bad stitching.

He had not waited long when the guard returned leading a middle-aged man in a green robe decorated with gold threaded embroidery tied with a silk sash around his waist. Shiro guessed this would be one of the lords of Nan. He stepped forward.

"I am lord Deshi," the man said. "I speak for the lords of Nan. Why are you here?"

Shiro gave a formal bow from the waist. "Well met, lord Deshi. I am Shiro of Liang. I come as an emissary of Emperor Shozun Maharant the third. I have been sent by Grandmaster Dalip to parlay with you."

Deshi spat to his side when he heard emperor Shozun's name. "He's no emperor of us. But very well, we will welcome you as an emissary. We're no barbarians here and we respect the rules of hospitality. We'll talk." He turned around and walked back into the castle.

Shiro felt lost. During his trip east he had imagined his reception. It had played out very differently in his head. There had been heralds and trumpets to announce him or perhaps a welcoming committee. Not this grumpy man who had allowed him into the fort with a couple of short sentences. He grabbed the reins of his horse and hurried after the man through the gatehouse.

The inside of the fort was very different from the grandeur of the Forbidden City. A handful of sandstone buildings sat around the cobbled courtyard. A pack of black guard dogs formed a sharp contrast with the red sandstone as they dozed on the far end of the courtyard. A multi-tiered keep with steep roofs stood against the far wall. Shiro didn't see any windows on the ground floor buildings, only arrow slits. A group of soldiers was having a drink at long tables near the keep.

Lord Deshi turned around and pointed at one of the low buildings next to the gatehouse. "Put your horse away in the stables, one of the hands will see that he's fed. After that, we'll find you a room in the keep." He set off across the courtyard.

Shiro headed towards the building lord Deshi had indicated, the clipping of the horse's hooves breaking the silence of the fort. He was almost at the double doors of the stable when the dogs started baying and charged towards him.

The horse reared up on its hind legs at this assault and pulled the reins out of his hand. Shiro shrank back against the stable walls, his heart racing, but the dogs seemed more focused on the horse. His luggage fell out of his saddle bags and scattered all over the courtyard.

A stablehand came running at the noise. When he saw the dogs, he gave a shout. He gave one of the dogs a thump and grabbed another by the collar and dragged it away from the horse. This subdued the dogs a bit. Shiro grabbed the reins again and forced its head away from the dogs. He stroked the horse's nose and whispered calm words to the horse.

"Sorry about that," the stablehand said. "I don't know what got into them. Let me take your horse, then you can gather your belongings." The boy gave the dog a final shove and walked over to the horse.

Shiro pulled his saddle bags from the horse and gathered his scattered luggage from the courtyard while the stablehand led the horse away. Closest lay some clothes, as did a cracked ink jar. The accompanying set of pens had rolled over towards the stable. The small box Grandmaster Dalip had given him lay towards the center of the courtyard. The lid was cracked and the stone that had been set in it was missing. Fortunately, the contents of the box had not spilled.

The stable hand appeared again, carrying Shiro's other bag. "Your horse is all set for the night."

"Thank you." Shiro dug out a couple of coins from his pocket and pressed them into the stablehand's hand. He grabbed his bags and headed over to the keep.

The ground floor of the keep had a military feel. The central corridor was just wide enough for one man to walk through at a time. Shiro stopped at the first room he passed and looked in. It was a guard room with racks of weapons along the wall. A couple of soldiers sat playing cards at a round table in the middle of the room.

Shiro cleared his throat. "Excuse me." The guards looked up from their game. "I am looking for Lord Deshi. He said I could find him here."

"He mentioned you'd show up. He told us to send you up to the third floor," the closest guard said. "You'll find the stairs down the hall on your left. Aran, the steward should be around to point you to your room."

On the third floor, Shiro was greeted by Aran, a short, middle aged man with a twirly moustache. Aran took over his bags and showed him to a narrow room with a single bed, desk and chair.

After promising to light a fire, Aran directed Shiro to the second floor. The rooms on the second floor were homelier. He found him on the second floor in the third room he checked. Lord Deshi stood with two other men close to the fireplace at the end of the room. The wooden floor was covered in reed mats and a small fire burned in the hearth. A low table next to the windows overlooked the courtyard. One of Lord Deshi's companions was short and broad, with his hair tied back in a warrior's knot. The other looked average in most ways, except for a very bushy moustache.

Lord Deshi looked up as Shiro entered. "Ah yes, the emissary. Come in and let me introduce you to Lord Delun." The short man nodded. "And this is Lord Takama." Lord Deshi pointed at the other man.

Shiro gave the men a bow. "Good evening masters, I am Shiro of Liang. I have been sent as emissary of Emperor Shozun Maharant the third by Grandmaster Dalip to treat with you. The Grandmaster wants to prevent unrest in the province and prevent unnecessary bloodshed."

Lord Delun snorted. "He just wants to buy us off and make us disappear."

"There now," lord Takama said. "He's just the messenger. Let's hear him out." He turned to Shiro. "What is Grandmaster Dalip's gracious offer?"

"The three of you will get an estate around the city of Tilgit in the province of Naipur worth three thousand sovereigns per year."

Lord Takama nodded. "That is a very gracious offer by the Grandmaster. And what's the other side of the coin. What does he want in return?"

"You must renounce the false emperor," Shiro continued. "And you must declare that anyone who follows him is a traitor to the one true emperor and to the empire."

"That is about what I expected," Lord Takama said.

After the strange welcome, this was going much better than expected. They saw how generous this offer was. Surely they would accept.

"We just have to denounce this false emperor and sacrifice everyone who has sided with us and we become rich in the process," Lord Takama continued. Shiro nodded. "I'm afraid we can't do that."

Shiro gasped and took a step back. This was not how it was supposed to go. Grandmaster Dalip had made a generous offer to settle this without bloodshed. "Don't just throw it all away," he said. "Please consider the offer some more."

"We have already," lord Deshi said. "We knew someone like you would come with an offer from the Forbidden City. And when we declared ourselves for the one true emperor, we agreed not to accept your offer."

"But why?"

"The emperor on the Jade Throne is a false emperor," lord Deshi said. "Having a pretender on the throne disturbs the cosmic balance and puts the whole empire at risk. Just look at the Khaganate invasion. They would never dare attack us with the true emperor on the throne."

"How can you say that?" Shiro asked. "Emperor Shozun is the rightful emperor and has been since he ascended the throne seven years ago."

"The emperor is a fraud, just as his father was a fraud," Lord Deshi said. "Emperor Isamo's son, Ozusho, died at birth, which left him without an heir. The throne should have passed to Isamo's brother Jiro. Instead, the Ministers put some imposter on the throne."

"How do you know? That must have been fifty years ago."

"Indeed, it was forty-seven years ago," Lord Deshi said. "And we know because we have talked to the mid-wife who delivered the still-born child of Emperor Isamo. She was tasked with hiding the child. When the baby Ozusho was shown to the public, they used the baby boy of one of the Ministers as a stand in."

Shiro felt lost. "But, it can't be. Emperor Shozun sits on the throne."

"Tell me," Lord Deshi took on a fatherly tone, "have you ever seen Emperor Shozun? Not just someone on the throne, but the actual emperor?"

The image of how he'd walked into the throne room came to mind, masked and dressed up, and how he'd sat on the jade throne in front of the Khaganate delegation. He dropped his head and spoke at the feet of the lords. "It's sacrilege to look upon the heavenly face of the emperor."

"Yes indeed. That's what I would say as well if I instituted a puppet emperor." Lord Deshi smiled. "I know it's a lot to take in. Think it over for a night. For now, please join us for diner." Lord Deshi gave a small bell that stood on the mantle a ring.

A moment later two servants walked in, each bearing a tray full with steaming food. They dished out steaming bowls with chicken and vegetable broth, flavored with lemongrass. There was pepper and cinnamon cooked beef and a dish of cabbage stir-fried with garlic and ginger. The smells reminded Shiro that he hadn't eaten since lunch time.

Shiro took some time while eating to collect his thoughts. The lords of Nan asked some polite questions about how Shiro's trip had been and what the latest gossip from the capital was.

Shouts and sounds of battle erupted in the courtyard. All four of them jumped up and ran for the windows to see what was happening outside. A figure was attacking the guards near the gatehouse. It was easily twice the height of the guards. It grabbed one of the guards and used him as a club to smash the other guards. The creature ripped off an arm of the guard it was holding and dropped him to the ground.

Behind the demon, more guards streamed out of the keep below Shiro. One of them had brought a bow and shot the creature in the middle of its back. The monster staggered forward. It let out a loud roar and turned around. The demon charged right at the guards near the keep, running on hands and feet. A second arrow took it in the shoulder but this hardly slowed the monster down as it crashed into the soldiers.

"We've got to help them!" Lord Delun shouted. He ran to the door.

"Stop," Lord Takama grabbed his arm as he passed. "We'll just get slaughtered like the guards!" He ran over to the door and barred it shut.

The fight had disappeared out of sight below the windows. They could hear the sound of bodies hitting the wall and the thump of iron hitting something. And then the sounds stopped. Silence descended on the fort. They looked out of the windows. Nothing moved in the courtyard. They waited in silence. Shiro counted to one hundred in his head.

Lord Delun was the first to speak. "I'm going down to see what's going on." He unlocked the door and tiptoed down the hallway. Shiro followed after him. They snuck down the stairs.

On the ground floor the guard rooms on both sides of the hallway were empty. The door outside at the far end stood half open. Lord Delun grabbed a short sword from one of the weapon racks in a guard room. Shiro followed his example. The sword felt unnatural in his hand. He gave it a couple of waves and almost dropped it. Still, it felt good to have something in his hands with which he could hit something.

They snuck through the hallway, swords held at the ready in front of them. At the door, they peered round the courtyard. Nothing moved outside. They stepped outside. Shiro gagged at the sight he saw. He covered his mouth with his hand. Soldiers lay in piles, limbs at odd angles. Blood covered their uniforms and was splattered around the courtyard.

"Go check to see if anyone is alive," Lord Delun said, waving right. He himself went left round the courtyard, examining the soldiers as he went.

Shiro approached the closest group of soldiers. He saw from a distance that they were all dead. Many had their necks broken, had pieces of flesh torn out or were missing limbs. He continued on. A bit further he saw that the demon, or whatever it had been, had even killed the guard dogs which had assaulted Shiro earlier in the day.

He met up with Lord Delun near the gatehouse at the far end of the courtyard. "Did you find anyone alive?" Lord Delun asked.

Shiro shook his head. "No."

"Neither did I."

"Who could do such a thing?" Shiro asked.

"I was about to ask you the same question. What was that thing and how did you let it in?"

"Me?" Shiro gasped. "I had nothing to do with this. I was with you the whole time."

"I find it very coincidental that the night you show up we get raided by a demon."

"A demon? How would I get a demon in here? What would I gain from killing everything in the courtyard?"

"I don't know," Lord Delun said. "But I don't like it one bit. Let's go back inside. Takama is better at thinking than I am."

They crossed the courtyard back to the keep. Lord Delun kept Shiro in front of him. About halfway across, Shiro saw a stone shaped like a five-pointed star lying on the ground. It looked exactly like the one that had disappeared from the top of his little chest, except that this one was slate grey instead of jet black.

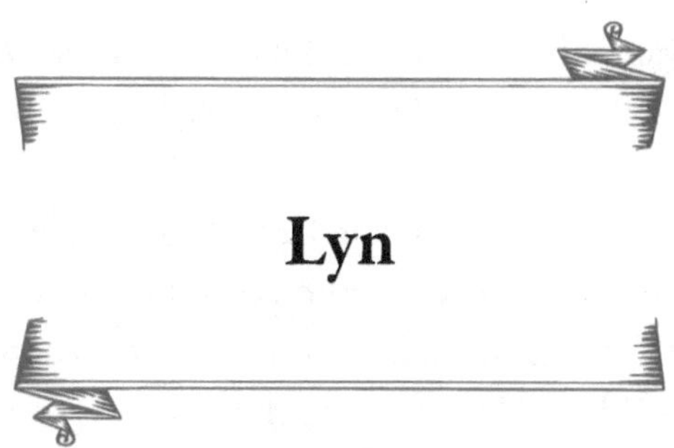

Lyn

The walls of Hinan and the Forbidden City appeared on the horizon. Shiro had remained for another day after the attack. The lords of Nan had clearly held him responsible for the demon attack, even if they didn't voice it out loud. As a result, the remaining negotiations had gone nowhere and Shiro had left dejectedly. He had spent most of the trip home pondering the words of the lords of Nan and the demon attack. He needed answers. During the whole trip he had considered the options available to him. And when the fields around Hinan first appeared he had reached a decision.

Asking Grandmaster Dalip or someone in the Ministry of Internal Affairs was not an option. If they gave him an answer at all, then he would be unable to tell if they were speaking the truth or not. And if the demon had really come from Grandmaster Dalip, as the lords of Nan believed, then asking questions would be dangerous.

As for the other masters and lords, they would either have no knowledge about what was going on and thus they would be unable to help him. Or they would know what was going on, in which case he would be in the same trouble as when he asked someone in the ministry directly.

There was only one person he could think of who might have answers. Lyn. She knew or suspected something about the ministry.

It was early afternoon when he rode into Hinan. Instead of riding straight ahead towards the Forbidden City he followed the wall to the right towards the fish market where he'd found Lyn last time. He made his way to the Smelly Cat, close to Lyn's house, stabled his horse there and got a room for the night. After dropping off his belongings, he continued on foot through the winding streets. He found a comfortable place to lounge from where he could observe Lyn's door. The small apartment looked empty. But then, she would probably be out at this time of day. Shiro settled in for a long wait.

Around him the shadows lengthened as the day drew to a close. The smells coming from the homes around him of people cooking diner made his stomach growl. He headed to a tavern he'd seen two blocks over. It was a cheap looking place, but at least the food was hot.

When he returned, a light was on in Lyn's apartment. He'd just missed whoever had come home. Damn. He had wanted to be sure that Lyn still lived there. What if Grandmaster Dalip had felt like tying up loose ends and Lyn had disappeared as well. And what if the grandmaster had guessed Shiro would come here to talk to Lyn. Then maybe one of Dalip's agents now lived there, waiting for him.

He needed to get a look through the window to see if Lyn still lived there. He walked around the block, looking for a better vantage point from where he could see into the apartment. He found nothing.

Shiro couldn't stay here in the street, walking back and forth much longer. Soon, someone would start asking questions.

If there was no easy stealth option to get a look then perhaps it was time for a different approach. He picked out a house across the street from Lyn's apartment and knocked on the door. He drew himself up to his full height, clasped his hands behind his back and waited for someone to answer the door.

An elderly man opened the door a crack. Shiro could see some wisps of grey hair around a narrow face. "Wha'dya'wan?" He asked.

Shiro assumed his most official sounding voice. "Ministry of Internal affairs. I've got an inspection to run. Please let me enter."

"Inspection? I dunno about no inspection. "

"I am running the fire and safety inspection. And your residence has been selected for a check. You are allowed to refuse entry. But then you will have to come explain your reason for doing so to the magistrate. Your choice."

"All right, all right." The man opened the door further. "There's no need for threats. I don't want no trouble."

Shiro walked in past the old man. "Please wait here, sir. This should only take a moment," he said. He made a quick tour of the ground floor, making a show of checking things. Then he headed upstairs. The single room upstairs was filled with a sleeping mat which took up most of the space in the room. A bulky wardrobe filled most of the remaining space. He walked over to the window, careful not to step on anything, and looked out.

The window offered a clear view into Lyn's apartment. There was no one there.

"Everything all right, sir?" The old man called up. "I can come up for any questions."

"No, stay downstairs. Everything looks fine," Shiro answered. "I am just, uhm, inspecting."

He couldn't stay here much longer. He heard the old man downstairs walk towards the stairs. Any moment now he would have to leave.

He saw shadows move around Lyn's room again. Someone was walking towards the window. Lyn walked into view. There was no doubt about it. Even at this distance he saw a hint of her green eyes. He turned from the window and walked out of the room just as he heard the old man come up the stairs.

"I have seen all I need," he said to the old man. "Everything is in order. Thank you for your cooperation. I will make sure to note in my report how helpful you have been."

Out in the street, Shiro thought about his options. At least Lyn still lived there. Now the question was how he would get her to talk to him. She wouldn't let him in. She had made that very clear last time. But if he got into her room, he'd have time to explain things. He walked past her house and in to a small alley a few doors down.

Initially, the alley had blank walls on either side. But, maybe halfway down, the house on Lyn's side was replaced with a wall, fencing off the back gardens between the houses. Shiro jumped and pulled himself up until he could look over the wall. The first garden had a small vegetable plot out back. He couldn't see anything in the second garden. In the third garden a plum tree grew up to the roof of the houses. He might just be able to use that to climb into the window at the back of Lyn's apartment.

He dropped back down and looked around for something he could use to get a leg up over the fence. He dragged some rocks and a crate into a pile and placed a foot on top, testing it for stability. When the pile stayed in place, he walked a few steps back, took a run and pushed off the pile. He pulled himself to the top of the wall and slung over his leg. He dropped down into the first garden and stayed low, looking around to see if he had been spotted. When there were no shouts, he hurried across the little garden to the next wall.

In this way, he made his way across the gardens until he stood underneath the plum tree. His guess from the alley had been correct. Some of the lower branches would let him reach Lyn's window. He grabbed the highest branch he could reach, put one foot against the trunk and with a quick hop made it into the tree.

He shuffled over to the window. A glance told him no one was around to notice him. He took out his dagger and worked the window frame until he could lift the latch. He gently pulled open the window. He swung his feet over the window sill and dropped to the floor without making a sound.

He straightened and was hit in the back of his head by some heavy object.

Shiro dropped to the floor, rolled into a ball and put his arms protectively around his head. "Please don't hit me," he pleaded.

"You?" Lyn's voice sounded incredulous. "I knew the ministry couldn't be trusted."

Shiro peeked around his arm. Lyn stood over him with a chopping board held high. "Please don't hit me," he repeated. "I'm not here for the ministry."

"You'd better have a very good reason to break in here then."

"I need to know about Poshu." Shiro dropped his voice to a whisper. "I need help."

This seemed to calm Lyn. She lowered the chopping board. "Get up." She waved her chopping board to a chair and table standing on the other side of the room. "Sit."

Shiro staggered to the chair. "Talk," Lyn said. "What is going on?"

Shiro started talking. He told her about what the lords of Nan had told him and about the demon attack. Lyn let him talk without interruption.

"But what is the problem," she asked when he had finished. "Why does it matter to you who the emperor is?"

"It's not just that." Shiro looked at his hands. "I'm afraid. I'm afraid of what would have happened if the demon would have been released in the dining room with the lords of Nan. There was nothing left alive in that courtyard. The demon had even killed a random mouse that happened to be around. He would have killed me."

Lyn let out a small sigh. "Do you know why you were chosen to join the ministry?" her voice had softened.

"Yes. Grandmaster Dalip told me. They were impressed with my performance and wanted to give me the next step in my career."

Lyn laughed. "It does sound great like that. No, you weren't chosen because you are so amazing, although they do like smart people. You were chosen because you're expendable."

"No." Shiro shook his head. "That can't be right."

"Let me guess." Lyn put her hand against her lips in thought. "You're from a small village somewhere out in the province. From your accent I'd guess Kaira somewhere."

"From Liang."

"I knew it. Your parents are some simple tradesmen, if they are still alive that is. Something like a merchant or innkeeper. You're a third or fourth kid."

"How do you know?"

"Because you're all like that. Poshu was from some backwater town in Naipur. He had a friend from Jaira whose hometown was so small it didn't even have a proper name. You all have similar stories. No one will miss you when you disappear. No one important at least."

"What do I do?" Shiro asked.

Lyn's laugh rang clear through the room. "I don't know sweetie. You can either run or you can accept it and hope you survive."

"They'll never let me go." Shiro shook his head.

"Well, then you'd better learn how to survive."

"What actually happened to Poshu?"

The smile disappeared from Lyn's face. "I don't know. He just disappeared. Like you, he had grown afraid of the ministry. On a few occasions he barely managed to survive a mission. So, he wanted out. We decided to run off together. We had made our plans. And then, days before we would leave, he simply vanished."

"I'm sorry to hear that."

"So am I."

There seemed nothing left to say after this. Shiro got up. "Thank you."

"I'm sorry about hitting you in the head."

"It's all right."

Dire tidings

Shiro stood against the wall at the back of the imperial reception room, hands clasped behind his back. Today the emperor was overseeing a dispute between two minor provincial lords. Shiro thought back to the suffocating mask and too warm outfit. He was glad it wasn't him. Besides being uncomfortable, it was also a lot harder to listen in on what was being discussed at the back of the reception room. Shiro wondered which of his colleagues from the ministry wore the imperial mask today. It might be Renshu, or maybe Tang. They both had some job to do down in the city today. It certainly wasn't Ray, since he was standing across the room, no doubt listening to what the entourage of Lord Pirun discussed.

Presently, Lord Hiro was explaining why Lord Pirun needed to pay toll for passing with his army over Lord Hiro's lands, and how the soldiers had ruined the roads with their heavy carts and been mean to the local peasants.

Dalip himself oversaw the proceedings, glaring at the lords any time they took a verbose detour in their story. It had an unsettling effect on the two lords, who kept making their exchanges shorter and shorter. He seemed very impatient today. Normally he was diplomatic and patient with the nobles from around the empire. Something had to be wrong.

The door to the reception room opened and a messenger walked in. He still wore his woolen travel cloak and riding boots, his brown message bag strapped across his shoulders. He must have come here as soon as he arrived at the palace, without stopping to freshen up. And barging in like that, it had to be an urgent missive.

Shiro wondered what it could be about. The messenger whispered to a lackey near the door. Shiro shuffled over to catch what the messenger was saying, but Lord Pirun's high pitched voice defending his soldiers made it hard to make out anything. The lackey raised a hand to his mouth, his eyes widening. It had to be something bad.

When the messenger stopped talking, the lackey walked forward, his whole pose indicated that he wanted to run. He reached Dalip and whispered something in Dalip's ear. Dalip nodded as the messenger finished and stepped away.

Dalip raised his hand and cut into lord Hiro's speech. "I've heard enough. We decree that lord Pirun has to pay toll for the usage of the road in the amount of half a penny per soldier." Whispering at this rushed verdict sprang up around the room. "We are adjourned for the rest of the day." He got up and walked to the door to his study at the side of the reception room.

Lord Hiro took several quick steps towards Dalip. "Grandmaster, I haven't finished my plea yet."

Dalip rounded on the lord. "The verdict has been spoken." Suppressed anger sounded in his voice.

"But Grandmaster," lord Hiro said, ignoring the threat that sounded in Dalip's voice. "Half a penny is much too little in compensation for all the damages."

"Do you question the divine will of the emperor? To do so is treason."

Lord Hiro turned white. "No, no, Grandmaster. Of course not. I was just surprised."

Dalip turned and walked out of the room.

As soon as Dalip had left the room everyone started talking. Something had to be seriously wrong for Dalip to leave this suddenly, without even waiting for the emperor to leave the room. The herald near the throne caught on and started the ceremonial declamation to indicate the emperor leaving. "Emperor Shozun Maharant the third has spoken in judgment. Bask in the wisdom of the conqueror of nations, the vanquisher of demons, and the bringer of dawn." All in the room fell to their knees. The emperor got up and headed for the door.

The imperial reception room was in disarray. The two petitioners were talking with a lot of arm waving amongst their retainers. As the lackeys opened the doors to let everyone exit, the next group of petitioners walked in, only to be told their petition had been cancelled for some unknown reason. Shiro took in the whole scene, trying to remember as much of it as possible. Master Jin was bound to ask about it later today.

A servant approached the messenger, who still stood by the door. Shiro caught the words Grandmaster Dalip. The messenger followed the servant out of the reception room. On an impulse, Shiro headed after them. He might learn more about what had just happened.

The servant took the messenger straight to Dalip's study. Shiro snuck in after them and took up a place along the wall. He leaned casually against one of the bookcases and pretended he'd been standing there the whole time already. Grandmaster

Dalip stood at his desk, with Master Jin and general Akira sitting in the chairs opposite him. The messenger stood between them, facing Dalip. Next to the doorway at the far end of the room Ray and Renshu leaned against the wall in a pose similar to Shiro's.

Dalip was the first to talk. "I need the whole message."

The messenger bowed. "Yes, Grandmaster," he placed a scroll on the desk. "General Tengfei has sent me. He had received a message from the Khaganate. They sent a horse with Maruf tied to his back. The gold he had received had been melted and poured over him, and two of the rubies in our gift had been set in place of his eyes. They added a message to the display. It read that this is the way they returned the treasure the traitor had received in payment for the peace treaty. And with the return of this payment they considered the treaty null and void."

"They invaded two days later. General Tengfei fended off the first assault, but he was later pushed back to the Eagle Pass. There he dug himself in. When I left him six days ago he was still holding out. He wants to inform you that the Khaganate has come in full force. He can hold out for a short time in the Eagle Pass, but he needs reinforcements and supplies. And he also can't protect all the other routes, should the Khaganate decide to travel south round the Kushal range."

Dalip picked up the scroll. "Very well, thank you for your message," he said. "You may go and get freshened up now."

The room was silent while the messenger left. Dalip looked at each of them in turn. "This is a situation. What are our options?"

Master Jin rubbed his chin. "I don't think we can buy them off. They are out for blood now. We need to face them on the field of battle."

"We can't face them in a straight fight," general Akira said. "And we need time to raise our armies as well. We're unprepared for a war."

"Yes, hence why we bought them off the first time," Dalip said.

"We don't have a choice," Master Jin said. "We have a war on our hands, whether we like it or not."

Dalip clasped his hands behind his back and paced back and forth. "So it seems indeed. But we don't have to make it a fair fight."

"What do you have in mind?" Master Jin asked.

Dalip walked over to the bookshelf in the corner and took out a leather bound tome from the top shelf. He placed in on his desk with a thump and flipped it open. "There are a lot of miles between here and the Kushal range." He leafed through the book, looking for a specific page. "And an army on the march is hungry, and, above all, very thirsty." He had found the page he was looking for. It showed an image of a metallic rock with a green shine to it, surrounded by a description. "We will poison all water supplies along the routes between the Kushal range and Hinan. If they attempt to cross the plains they will either go thirsty or suffer from the poisoning."

"What of the people living in that region? " Master Jin asked. "They need that water to survive as much as the Khaganites do."

"Their sacrifice for the empire will be remembered." Dalip said.

"We can at least warn them," general Akira said.

"No," Dalip said. "If we do so then the Khaganites will know something is up. And the bodies will be a source for diseases, which will add to the Khaganites' problems when crossing the plains."

Dalip looked first at Ray and Renshu, and then at Shiro. "Don't think I hadn't noticed you three. You will do this mission. The survival of the empire depends on it, you can not fail. And you can't tell anyone of this mission. We need the element of surprise to be as big as possible. And you never know who talks. Ray, you have the lead."

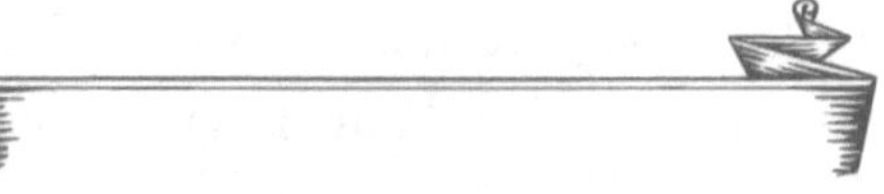

Making amends

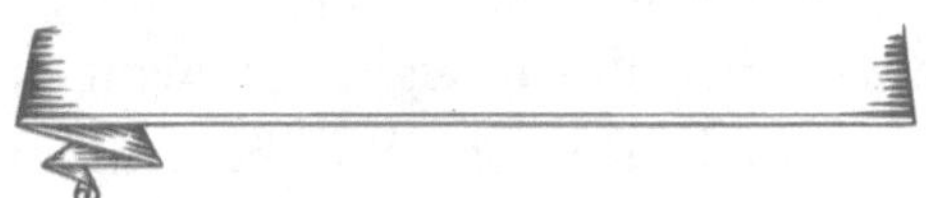

Shiro knocked on Taizo's door. The apartment building for the trade clerks felt very confined compared to the ministry building. He hopped from one leg to the other. He had not talked to Taizo since their falling out weeks ago. How would Taizo react?

"I'm coming." Taizo said from the other side of the door. "Who is it?" The door opened a crack.

"Hi," Shiro said.

Taizo paused for a moment when he saw Shiro. "What do you want?"

"I'm leaving in the morning," Shiro blurted out. He took a deep breath. "I mean, I wanted to apologize for the other night. And since I'm leaving on a trip tomorrow I decided to come now."

Taizo slapped Shiro's back. "It's alright." He flashed Shiro a smile. "Where are you going?"

"I can't say. Sorry."

Taizo's smile disappeared. "Some fancy, glamorous stuff us regular people can't know anything about I'm sure."

Shiro's stomach twisted in a knot when he imagined the poisoning mission. Very glamorous indeed. "No, it's nothing like that. Wait." He dug a sack out of his bag and held it up.

"This is the other reason I came. Each year, the Emperor has employees of the ministry hand out alms to the poor during the Linang festival."

"So you're going to play rich kid," Taizo said. "And you're here to rub my nose in it."

"No, that's not it at all. I thought you might like to help. It's not the most prestigious of jobs. But the ministry thinks well of people helping them."

Taizo's eyes lit up. "Sure I'll help. That's what friends are for. When do we start?"

"Follow me. We're heading to the fish market."

Two guards accompanied them to the fish market. The stalls had been cleared for the festival and a small platform had been set up on one end of the market square. People crowded in the market plaza, and their two guards had to shoulder their way through to get to the platform. They set up there and the people filed past. Each person received three copper coins, one for each of the rituals Linang had performed to create the moon.

Shiro looked over at Taizo. An old lady, dressed in rags hugged Taizo and shook his hand after she received her coins. The next, a man with a limp, gave him a bow. Taizo wore a grin from ear to ear and made some small talk with many of the people walking past. Shiro smiled. It was good to see his friend happy again.

The full moon was approaching her zenith when they finished. Around them the crowd dispersed.

Shiro and Taizo walked back to the Forbidden City in silence. Candles symbolizing the moon burned in the windows they passed.

"I think we made a lot of people happy tonight," Taizo said.

The walls of the Forbidden City, with the Ministry of Internal Affairs building in the middle of them, appeared ahead.

Shiro looked over at his friend. "We did good work. If you hadn't helped then I would still be out there." Shiro placed a hand on Taizo's shoulder. "Thank you."

They stopped underneath the ministry building.

"I had fun," Taizo said. "Let's go for a drink when you get back from your trip."

"Definitely." Shiro clasped Taizo's hand.

Out over the city, the moon reached her highest point. Ahead of them, fireworks went up, showering the Forbidden City in a rain of gold and red and green.

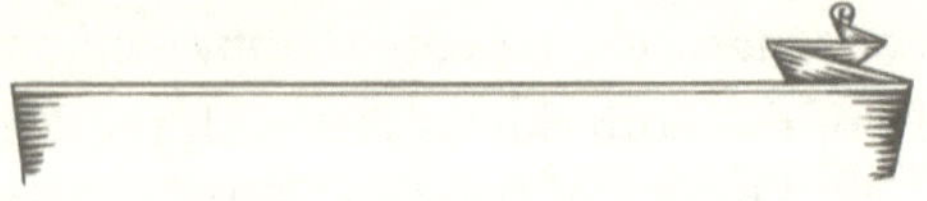

Poisoning the Khaganate

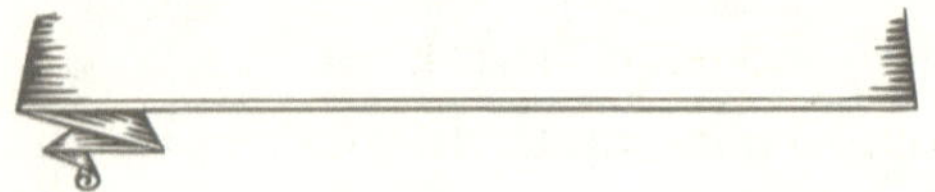

They had been on the road for a week when they came to a fork in the road. The shadows of the Kushal range spread along the horizon. To the south lay the town of Belu, while the road to the north-east ran on until the foothills of the Kushal range. Shiro stared at Ray's and Renshu's backs, as he had for the past couple of days. The saddlebags of his brown gelding were packed full with the poison they were tasked with spreading. Ray and Renshu were having some friendly banter about who was uglier.

Ray turned in his saddle. "Your target is south," he said to Shiro. "After Belu, continue on until you hit the caravan road from Urgan to Hinan. Travel two or three towns towards the border and from there, make your way back to Hinan. We'll continue on and cover the northern and central part of the range."

"Does it bother you at all?" Shiro asked Ray, "that we'll poison half a province."

"We do what needs to be done to protect the empire. The emperor has commanded it."

"For the empire," Renshu said.

Shiro gave a weak salute with his arm across his chest. He directed his horse down the side road. The poison grew in his mind as he rode through the empty landscape. He felt it burn against his legs through the saddlebags.

The sun indicated it was mid-afternoon when Shiro passed the first field. He was getting closer to Belu. The first soy fields and plum orchards showed by the side of the road. Belu itself appeared around a bend in the road. The village had sprung up in the shelter of a cliff, where an enterprising innkeeper had dug a well and built his inn. The village had grown around it. The houses were thick walled and low, offering some protection against the heat of the day.

The well sat in the middle of the plaza in front of the inn. A jujube tree, heavy with fruit, shaded the area. Two kids ran past, chasing some imaginary monster. A teenage girl drew a bucket of water and lugged it home.

Shiro decided to stay for a night. The next town was too far to reach before nightfall and poisoning the well in the middle of the day was a sure way to get noticed. He headed for the inn and booked a room.

NOTHING MOVED IN THE village and the moon was just rising when Shiro snuck out of the inn. He carried a cloth bag containing a lump of the grey metal. Thallium Dalip had called it. When dropped into a water source, it would slowly dissolve, giving off a tasteless poison. The lump he had was enough to spoil the well for the next four months at the least.

Shiro looked over the edge of the well. Stars sparkled on the water down below, dancing on the surface. The metal felt heavy in his hand. He grabbed the metal tight. In his mind, he saw the girl draw water from the well again and use it to cook her dinner.

Shiro straightened. He couldn't do it. The whole village would die. Even the empire was not worth sacrificing these innocent people for. Besides, the Khaganite army would never come this way. They would stick to the caravan road leading to Hinan. They had no reason to visit these villages, which meant that using the poison here was a waste. He would do better to save it until later and make sure he had enough for those places where the Khaganate would come to. He turned and headed back to the inn.

Shiro had hardly slept when the sun rose on Belu the next morning. Bleary eyed he had a quick breakfast of eggs and sausage before gathering up his belongings and heading out. It was still cool, but the sun already promised a baking hot day ahead.

Over the next couple of days, Shiro passed through several more hamlets and villages on his way to the caravan road. In each of them, he couldn't bring himself to poison whatever water supply they had. The most likely route for the Khaganate wouldn't come close to these places, so Shiro convinced himself he did no harm to Dalip's plan by just passing them by.

On the caravan road he hit a larger town, Kaidu. Perhaps a thousand people called it home. In the inn he booked for the night, he heard rumors of the approaching Khaganite army. Apparently some troops had gotten around the Eagle Pass and were hurrying across the plains to the west. He was out of excuses now. The Khaganite army was coming here. The people who lived here would suffer either way, and he had to help defend the empire. He wandered through the city, noting the different wells and fountains. It felt like Liang, where he'd grown up. He had considered Liang, which had been about the same size, a huge metropolis until he had come to Hinan and the Forbidden City.

That night, Shiro snuck out of the inn. He made his way to the western edge of the town, as far away from his inn as he could. The first well he came to sat in a plaza near the western gate. He leaned on the edge of the well, poison in hand and stared down. The people here didn't deserve this. But he could stop the Khaganate here, help them win this war.

He sighed. He held out his hand over the well and let go of the poison.

Afterwards, he visited several more wells, dropping a piece of the metal in each of them. At the end of the night, Shiro estimated he had visited perhaps half of the city's water supplies.

The next day, Shiro wandered through Kaidu. Kids ran through the streets chasing stray dogs or each other. Women chatted as they walked down the streets on their way to the market.

Shiro sat in the shade of a tree in one of the quiet plazas of the city. He thought about how all the inhabitants were oblivious to the fate that was waiting for them.

Across the plaza a mother appeared with a small child, maybe three years old, on her arm. She headed to the well to draw some water. He pictured the little lump of thallium lying at the bottom, dissolving, giving off its poison. It was the only way to prevent the Khaganate from striking deep into the empire. The empire and the emperor were all that mattered. And yet, he had not seen the emperor command anything, only Grandmaster Dalip.

It wasn't right. Shiro jumped up and ran towards the lady. He reached her just as she had gotten the bucket up over the rim of the well. "Wait!" he shouted. The woman looked up, confused.

"Wait," he repeated. Shiro thought fast. "I heard the well is poisoned. The Khaganate sent some spies to infiltrate and spoil the water."

The woman eyed the water in the bucket she had just hauled up. She smelled it for a moment. "Smells like water to me. Looks like it too."

"It's a poison that doesn't smell or taste of anything."

"Sure. I can't smell or taste it, but it's bad for me." She used the bucket to fill her own container. "And how do you know this?"

"I," Shiro hesitated. He couldn't say too much without revealing his own role. He deflated a little. "I overheard some kids talking."

"You shouldn't believe everything you hear, son. Still, thanks for taking the trouble." The mother walked off with her kid and container full of water.

Shiro stood staring around helplessly. He was not sure how long the poison would need to give an effect. But he had to be gone by tomorrow morning at the latest. As soon as people fell ill the woman might talk and someone would connect the dots.

The next day he left through the west gate, towards the Khaganite Empire, as the sun appeared over the horizon. On his way out, he made sure to have a chat with the guard lounging at the gate.

He rode for an hour and then left the road. He circled back around Kaidu until he hit the road to Hinan again. That evening he was overtaken by a rider coming in haste from behind him. It meant one of two things; either a Khaganate army had come in sight of Kaidu or the poison was starting to take effect and the woman had talked.

When Shiro rode into the next town, Nathun, he found it in uproar. The horse which had passed him stood outside the inn in the main square. The inn looked crowded, with several people standing on the doorstep, listening in on what was happening inside.

Shiro approached one of the people standing outside. "What's happening?"

"The Khaganites have been poisoning the water supplies on this side of Kushal range. Apparently half of Kaidu has fallen ill."

"That sounds horrible. What about here? Has anyone fallen ill yet?"

"No, it seems that so far we're unaffected. But if the Khaganites are in Kaidu already, then we're next. We're now discussing if we need to leave or guard our water sources and wait for the emperor to send aid our way."

At least this meant that poisoning the people of Nathun would be impossible. "I wouldn't want to stay with a Khaganite army approaching," he said. "I heard they sacrifice people to their dark gods."

"Indeed," one of the men answered. "And I've heard it said that they eat the children of their enemies."

Others muttered in agreement. Shiro's remark quickly spread through the crowd. More and more voices went up to flee from the oncoming horde to the safety of the capital. In the end they agreed to post guards on the different water sources of the town and that they would leave the day after tomorrow.

Shiro decided to stick around. Poisoning the town's water sources would be impossible now that they were guarded. But after everyone left, doing so would be easy, and as a bonus no inhabitants would suffer from the poisoning.

TWO DAYS LATER THE whole town stood in the central square of Nathun. Richer inhabitants had piled as much of their belongings as would fit onto carts. Shiro saw everything from furniture to chickens. Other, less fortunate inhabitants carried stuffed backpacks on their backs. Kids bounded around the column, exited to be on a trip. Shiro left early morning and hid off the road, close to the town.

By mid-morning the last cart had passed Shiro on its way towards Hinan. He waited until mid-day before riding back to Nathun. Many of the doors and windows were boarded shut. The town was deserted. Shiro let out a sigh of relief. He rode past the different water sources and dropped a bit of the poison in each of them.

Back in the main town square he looked around. The small temple across the inn looked forlorn. Shiro wandered in. The local monks had taken the statues with them, but the smell of incense was still heavy in the air. Shiro knelt in front of where the main statue would have been. He prayed that he would be forgiven for what he had done and that the town would have a bright future ahead of it.

As he left the temple and mounted his horse he saw a dust cloud rise up on the horizon. The Khaganate were approaching.

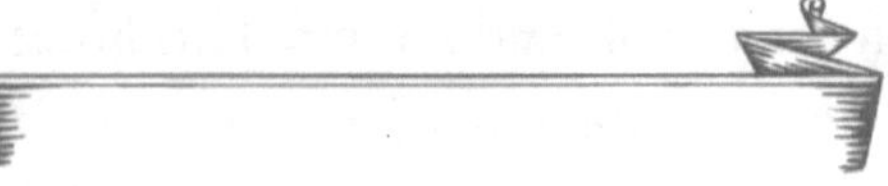

Back in Hinan

In the first few towns Shiro passed on his way back to Hinan there were still people around packing their belongings. Each time, Shiro waited until the town had emptied before poisoning the wells. After that, most towns were already abandoned by the time Shiro got to them, their inhabitants warned by faster riders. The stream of refugees grew until the road was full and everything moved at a snail's pace.

It took Shiro two-and-a-half weeks to make the return trip. All this time the dust cloud on the horizon grew. By the time the walls of Hinan appeared, the Khaganate army was on their heels. So much for slowing them down by poisoning the water sources along the way.

Shiro made his way through Hinan to the Forbidden City. Everywhere there were signs of military preparation. Patrols marched along the walls, supplies were being carted in through the city gates and refugees filled the streets and squares of the Hinan.

In the Forbidden City itself there were no refugees. The Imperial guards had made camp in the Plaza of the Five Dragons, near the main gate into the City. They questioned everyone trying to enter and only people on official business were admitted. They let Shiro pass without issue when he told them he worked in the Ministry of Internal Affairs and had an important missive for Grandmaster Dalip.

He dropped off his few belongings and made his way to Dalip's study. The Grandmaster would want a report. When Shiro was admitted to the study he saw that Master Jin, general Akira and Ray were already present. They stood around Dalip's desk looking down on a map of the empire. Various markers were scattered around the map.

"Welcome back Shiro," Dalip said. "It's good to see that two of you made it back. I think it's safe to assume by now that Renshu will not make it back to Hinan ahead of the Khaganite forces. How did your mission go?"

"I was successful in what I wanted to do. After leaving Ray and Renshu near Belu I visited all the wells I could find. I managed to poison all sources of fresh water I could find between here and Kaidu and I even rode beyond it towards the border with the Khaganate." There was no lie in there at least, even if it gave Dalip a different impression from what had really happened. "Unfortunately, a rumor spread somehow in Kaidu that the Khaganate had agents in the town and they had poisoned the town's wells. Riders from Kaidu warned the other cities along the caravan road. So perhaps the effect was less than you'd hoped."

"Hm." Dalip rubbed his chin. "It's a shame we lost the elements of surprise and disease. But there's nothing to be done about that anymore."

"I apologize, sir."

"You did well, given the circumstances. We need to look to the defense of the city now."

Dalip turned back to the map on the desk. He added a couple of markers to the different towns Shiro had mentioned to indicate poisoned water supplies. Shiro saw that Ray had managed to poison fewer towns on the road leading to Eagle Pass than he had. In Renshu's part, the Northern part of the Kushal range, no towns were marked.

Dalip pointed at two of the markers indicating the Khaganite armies. "Can we engage one of them in the field before they can join up?"

"In the best circumstances I wouldn't want to engage the Khaganites on equal ground," general Akira said. "As it stands, our army isn't ready for any real battle, let alone against a Khaganite cavalry charge. We need more time to raise and train our army."

"How do we gain time?" Dalip asked.

"Our best bet is to abandon the city and fall back with our army," General Akira said, "probably either to Nan or to Kaira. That way, we can stay ahead of the Khaganites, recruit more troops and make a stand at a more defensible place."

"Abandon the Forbidden City? Out of the question! We will not abandon the imperial seat just because some barbarians have shown up."

"Then we need to slow down their march," general Akira said. "Poisoning the water supplies has already helped in that regard. And all the fugitives on the road will slow them down as well."

"Are there other options?" Dalip asked.

Master Jin spoke up. "If we can break their chain of command then we should slow them down, with the added benefit that they will be less fearsome in combat if they are missing their leaders."

"How would you manage that?" General Akira asked. "You just want to walk into their camp, ask for their officers and kill them?"

Grandmaster Dalip steepled his fingers. "No, of course not. That would be suicide. We couldn't get a human close enough to their officers to get any result. Of course, sacrifices have to be made, but not by sending soldiers to their deaths on a futile mission. What other options do we have?"

"We could send harrying forces to keep them occupied," General Akira said.

"We can't spare them," Master Jin said.

"Agreed," Dalip said. "For now, send out scouts to find out as much as we can about their movement and troop composition. Let's think about other options we have and convene again tomorrow."

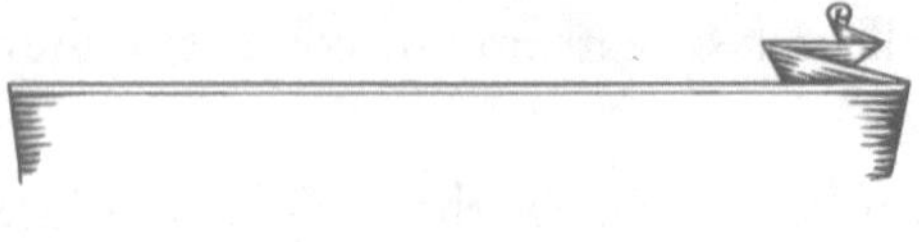

Sacrifices

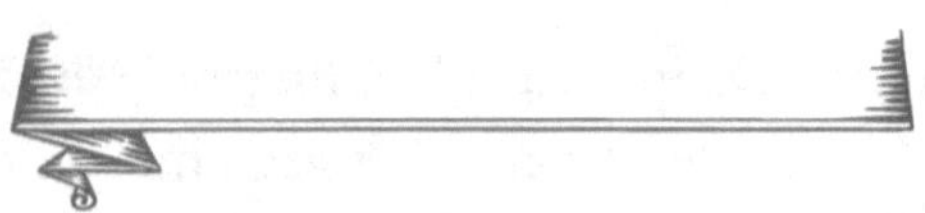

"Don't go," Shiro said to Taizo.

"Why?" Taizo asked.

They stood on the edge of the Forbidden City, close to the trade department and Shiro's old apartment building. The setting sun painted the sky in red and purple. The grey clouds on the horizon promised rain somewhere tomorrow or the day after.

Shiro thought back to Dalip's words about sacrifices. He didn't want his friend to become entangled in the grandmaster's schemes. "I'm not sure. But I believe it will be dangerous."

"That's bullshit. You're just jealous that they asked me for help instead of you. Suddenly you're not so special anymore." Taizo turned away from Shiro and headed down the street.

"Wait," Shiro hurried after him. "Please don't go. The ministry isn't as amazing as it seems."

"If you think that, then why don't you leave?"

Shiro saw himself sitting on the jade throne, wearing the imperial mask. "I can't," he mumbled.

"We are done with this discussion." Taizo made a dismissive gesture with his arm. "I am going. This is my ticket to move up in the world. If you want to deny me that then you're no true friend. We're done here." Taizo walked off.

Shiro stood staring after him, at a loss. He had been having dinner with Taizo, catching up after Shiro's trip, when a messenger had come with a summons from Dalip. Taizo had felt excited; sure that Grandmaster Dalip had great plans for him.

Shiro had remembered Lyn's comment about being expendable. He had tried to talk Taizo out of going, but Taizo had already had his mind made up.

To Shiro, something felt off about this summons, like an itch in the middle of his back he couldn't quite reach. Why would Dalip send for anyone at this hour? It must be something urgent, given the time of day, but the only urgent matter that came to mind was the war. And how would someone from outside the Ministry of Internal Affairs be of use there? Especially a simple clerk from the Trade Department like Taizo.

Shiro decided to spy on Taizo to see if he could learn anything. Since he knew where Taizo was headed, Shiro decided to take a few short cuts through several buildings. That way, Taizo couldn't notice him and get suspicious. As he entered the second building he realized he was taking the exact same route as he had all those weeks ago when he had first followed Master Chin to Dalip's study. The guards recognized him as a member of the Ministry of Internal Affairs and ignored him as he ran past.

The last of the daylight had disappeared when Shiro came to the plaza in front of the Imperial Quarter. Only one or two people walked across the plaza. Strange. At this time of day there should have been at least a handful of guards around. He hurried across the plaza to the side of the Imperial Quarter. The side entrance here gave access to the imperial wing where Dalip had his study. It offered a less conspicuous entrance into the Imperial Quarter and one from where he could more easily watch Dalip's study.

Voices echoed through the corridor as Shiro approach Dalip's study. Dalip and Taizo were talking in the atrium.

Shiro glanced around the corner into the atrium. Apart from Dalip and Taizo it was deserted. They stood in front of the doors of the throne room. Their voices echoed through the silent building. Dalip had apparently been waiting in the atrium for Taizo and they were already past introductions by the time Shiro could make out what was being said.

"The emperor needs you," Dalip said. "He needs you to aid the empire in this hour of need."

"I will do whatever it takes to serve his Holiness," Taizo said.

"I knew I could count on you. When we discussed candidates for this mission, your name came up. And I told the emperor you would not disappoint him."

Shiro shuddered. This sounded too much like what Dalip had told him when he'd first joined the ministry.

"What do you need me to do?" Taizo asked.

"We'll get to that in good time, my son. Before I take you to the emperor you must promise me that you will stay strong. Your nerves will be tested. But if you stay true then you will save the empire."

"I promise. The emperor can count on me."

"I knew we could count on you." Dalip placed a hand on Taizo's shoulder. "Your sacrifices will be remembered and you will be greatly rewarded for your service. Follow me."

Dalip led Taizo round the left of the throne room, towards the imperial apartments. Shiro darted across the atrium as soon as they disappeared round the corner. He made it just in time to see Dalip and Taizo pass into the imperial bedchamber.

By the time Shiro got there, the bedchamber was dark and empty. No one slept in the imperial bed straight across from the door. The doors on either side of the room stood closed. Shiro cursed. There was no time to search through the different rooms and if he accidentally ran into someone he would have a hard time explaining what he was doing here. He looked around. Where had they gone?

A flicker of light in the hearth drew his attention. Shiro hurried over. The light flickered through a narrow opening in the side of the hearth. The sound of footsteps came through the opening.

He squeezed through the opening. The passage on the other side ran for a couple of steps to a flight of stairs leading down, a single torch burning a few steps down. This was the flicker Shiro had seen.

Shiro tiptoed down the stairs and came to a dark, silent room. Some type of crates lay scattered around the room. He hurried back up the stairs and grabbed the torch hanging from the wall.

When he got back down the stairs, the light from the torch glittered off pieces of gold and precious stones lying in chests around the room. He had found the fabled imperial treasury.

Where had they gone? There was only one way into the room and he had just come down it. Shiro leaned against the far wall, torch in hand.

He stood for a moment, hand in his hair, looking around.

A draft wafted past his head. Shiro held up his torch. The flame flickered in the draft. Shiro ran his hand over the wall. A small gap ran along the wall just above his head. Shiro pushed against the wall. A part of the wall swung inward. Shiro held his breath, listening. His heart raced.

Shiro counted to thirty. He released his pent up breath when no one showed up and slowly eased open the door further. Another flight of stairs ran straight down for twenty odd steps and then made a sharp turn.

He left his torch in the treasury and started down the stairs. He realized that they would take him to right underneath the throne room. Voices came up from down below. One was definitely Dalip's, but some of the others were harder to make out.

An otherworldly vista spread out as he rounded the corner. The stairs ran down another fifty feet into a large cavern. Torches burned along rough stone walls, a draft causing the shadows to dance all across the cavern, creating an otherworldly glow. A raised altar stood in the center of the room in the middle of a five-pointed star, similar in shape to the stone Dalip had given him for his trip to Nan. Dalip and Taizo and two people Shiro didn't recognize stood in front of the altar, looking down on three other hooded and cloaked people who stood in a semi-circle below the altar.

Shiro snuck down to the floor level of the cavern and hid in a corner next to the stairs.

Dalip started talking again. "Since we're all in agreement, let us begin." He turned around to the altar and picked up a bone-white knife. "With the blood of the people we bridge the divide." His voice threw echoes off the walls. With a quick jab, he pricked his finger. Slowly, a drop of blood oozed out and fell on to the altar with a sizzle like a drop of water hitting a burning hot pan. Another drop oozed out and fell, and a third.

At the third hiss, black smoke rose up twenty feet from the altar. It writhed around and around, forming into a ball and then flattening. A voice like nails being drawn over a slate tile came out of the cloud. "Who calls?" The hair on Shiro's arms stood up at the voice.

Dalip and the three hooded figures dropped to their knees. "We are the humble servants and protectors of the empire," they intoned. "We call upon you to aid us in our need."

The surface of the cloud cleared up as if it had turned into a window. A horned face looked down on them. It reminded Shiro of the demon head carved into the emperor's door leading into the throne room. Intelligent yellow eyes looked at the seven men in front of him. Curved fangs framed a mouth full of pointed teeth. "What need do you have?" The face asked.

Grandmaster Dalip spoke into the floor. "We are beset by the Khaganate Empire. We need help to take out the leaders of the three armies approaching the Forbidden City."

The demon seemed to be considering. "This can be arranged, for a price. Will you supply us with a portal stone?"

"No," Dalip answered. "We cannot get close enough to deliver the stone. I have brought a map indicating where the armies can be found." Dalip placed a scroll on the altar. It sizzled like a slice of meat on a grill and disappeared.

"I see." The demon stroked his chin. "We will need three willing to make the sacrifice in that case."

Dalip rose up to sit on his knees. He indicated the three men standing around him. "I have brought them, great one. They have all indicated they are willing to do whatever it takes for the empire."

"I need to hear it directly from them."

Dalip got up and walked to Taizo. "This is your moment to shine. Tell him what you told me earlier."

"I-." Taizo hesitated. He swallowed and continued. "I will do whatever it takes to serve the empire."

Dalip repeated this ritual with the other two men standing near the altar.

"Very well," the demon said. "The payment is accepted."

Dalip turned around to the three men and waved them up. Each of them stepped up and grabbed on to one of the men. The one furthest away from Taizo was directed forward. The hooded man pushed the victims head down on to the altar stone. Dalip walked up and with a quick slice opened up the victim's jugular vein. Blood splattered all over the altar and ran down its sides. The lines of the five-pointed star on the floor began to give off a soft glow. In the smoke cloud, the demon began licking his lips.

Shiro sat frozen in his place. "Taizo, no," he mouthed silently. He grabbed the edge of the staircase he was hiding under, squeezing until his knuckles turned white.

The second sacrifice was dragged forward. The man thrashed in the grip of the man holding him. Dalip repeated the process, the extra blood causing the star around the altar to glow brighter.

Shiro looked around for anything he could do to save his friend. Tears ran down his cheeks.

Taizo was forced down on the altar.

Shiro was frantic. The floor of the cavern was bare. There was nothing around to save Taizo.

Dalip raised the knife.

"No!" Shiro shouted.

The grandmaster dragged the knife across Taizo's neck and Taizo's blood ran over the altar.

The star on the floor started glowing bright white as Taizo's blood was added to the star. Dalip and the three men spun around at the shout. Dalip pointed. "Get him!"

The three men sprang forward. One of them was Master Jin. Up on the altar, Taizo's body slumped to the floor. This roused Shiro. If those men caught him, he would join Taizo's fate. He fled up the stairs two steps at a time.

When he reached the treasury he slammed the door shut and looked around for something to block the door with. There was nothing useful.

Desperate he grabbed the torch he'd left on the floor and wedged it in the gap above the door. It wouldn't hold them for long, but it was better than nothing.

Something crashed into the door on the other side. Shiro ran across the room to the stairs leading up to the imperial bedchamber. Behind him, the door groaned as it was being forced open. He fled through the bedchamber into the atrium. There he sprinted out of the Imperial Quarter and into the night.

There, the cold hit him after the oppressive heat of the cavern. He had made it out alive. But now what?

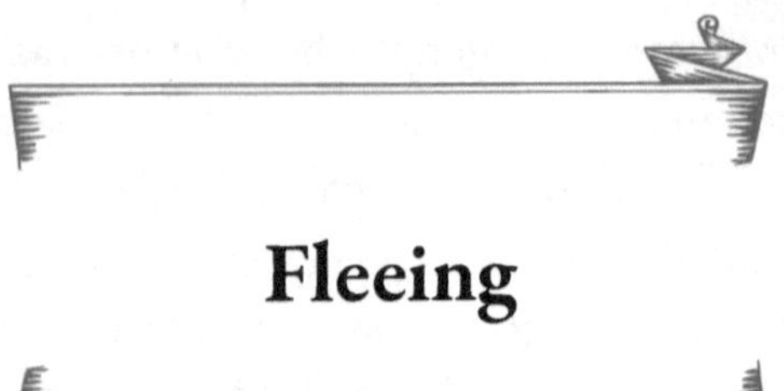

Fleeing

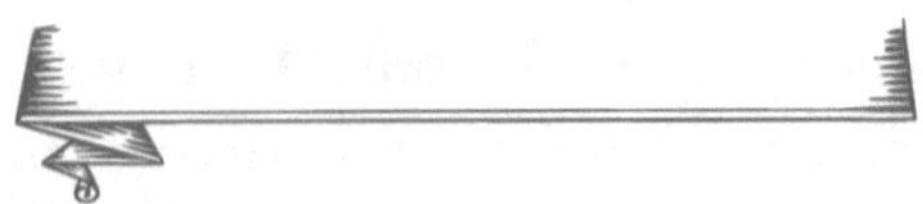

It was somewhere after midnight when Shiro pounded on Lyn's door.

"Yes, alright, I'm awake, I'm coming," Lyn said. "Who is it?"

"Please let me in."

"Shiro?" She asked through the door. "What are you doing here?"

"Please, hurry."

She opened the door a crack and looked out. When she saw that Shiro was alone she opened it a bit further. "What are you doing here?" She asked again. She was dressed in a nightgown. Shiro had woken her up.

Shiro pushed past her into her apartment.

"Hey. I didn't say you could come in."

Shiro walked into the living room and started pacing back and forth. "I'm sorry for showing up like this. I didn't know where else to go."

"Calm down. What's going on?"

Shiro walked over to the window and glanced out at the street. It lay empty. He walked to the other side of the room and sat on the floor. "I don't think anyone followed me."

"Followed you? Shiro, you're not making sense."

"I think I know what happened to Poshu. And I'm afraid it will happen to me too."

She grabbed Shiro by his shoulders and forced him to stand still. "What is going on, Shiro?"

Shiro looked her in the eye. "They killed him."

"Who?"

"Taizo. They just took him and sacrificed him, and now he's dead."

"Who is Taizo? Sit down and tell me everything." She directed Shiro over to her table and pushed him into a chair.

Shiro took a deep breath. "Taizo is my friend. Was my friend," Shiro corrected himself. "We came to the forbidden city together." He told Lyn what he had seen. When he came to Taizo's murder his voice broke.

"When they finished they spotted me. I ran," Shiro concluded. "I think I managed to delay them for long enough so they didn't see where I went. At first I just ran and ran, out of the Forbidden City. I took random turns left and right, just to make sure they couldn't catch me. Only when I reached the harbor did I slow down and start to think about my options. There were no ships leaving the city at this time of night. The first one to leave is bound for the City of Spires the day after tomorrow, and I have no money to pay for that trip. You were the only person I could think of who didn't live in the Forbidden City and who might help me. So I came here."

"I'm afraid of what will happen to me if they catch me." Shiro fell silent.

Lyn dropped down on the floor next to Shiro. "Finally I know," she said. "I always wondered if Poshu had run off without me or if he had been sent on a mission by the ministry." A tear ran down her cheek. "But now I know."

They sat in silence for a while. Shiro played the night's events back in his mind, wondering how he could have saved Taizo.

"What are you going to do?" Lyn asked.

Shiro looked up. "I don't know. My whole life is here. And if I go back to the Forbidden City they will take me and do to me what they did to Taizo."

"You can't stay here."

"I know. But I had nowhere else to go."

"You can stay for a night."

"Thank you. I will leave in the morning."

On the run

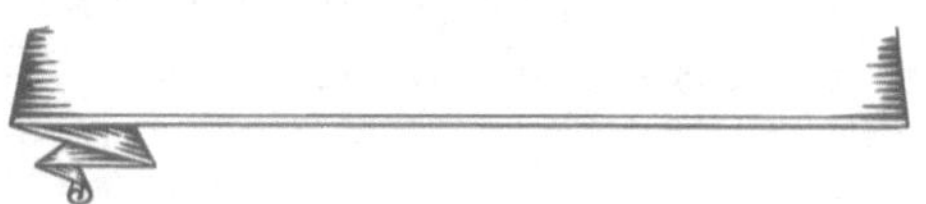

Shiro woke to the sound of breakfast being made. For a moment he lay with his eyes closed and thought he was at home and his mother was cooking. Then he remembered Taizo's death the previous night's events and he bolted upright.

Lyn walked into the small living room, carrying two plates of food. "Good morning," she said.

"Hi," Shiro answered.

"How do you feel? Did you get any sleep?"

"A little." Shiro rubbed his temples. "It all feels unreal. I need some time to process it all."

"Have you already figured out what you will do?" Lyn asked.

"I'm not sure yet." Shiro ran a hand through his hair. "I can't stay in Hinan. Here I'll eventually run in to someone I know and then Dalip will find me. So I'm leaving the city. But the question is, where to."

"Do you have any family you could go to?"

"My parents are still living in Liang, as are my brother and sister. But I fear that Dalip will send someone to check. If I go there they'll be in danger."

"Where to then?"

"I need a place where Dalip can't get to me. Somewhere where they won't think to look or where they can't."

"You mean some place foreign, like the Khaganate?" Lyn asked.

"Except that the Khaganate will probably not be feeling too generous towards staff from the Ministry of Internal Affairs."

Shiro tapped his finger against his lips. He went through all the places he could think of. "Maybe I can go to the lords of Nan and the other emperor."

"Who are they?"

"They're a group of Eastern lords who have found out that the emperor doesn't exist anymore, and they have tracked down someone who they then think is the rightful emperor, the grandson of the brother of the grandfather of the current emperor. They have no reason to like Dalip or betray me to the ministry, and Dalip can't just take a look in their court."

"Sounds like a plan," Lyn said.

"Let me help you with the dishes and then I'll be on my way." They gathered up the plates and headed in to the kitchen.

Shouts erupted in the street. Shiro ran over to the window. City guards marched down the street, pushing everyone aside. Down the road more guards were setting up a roadblock. They were coming here.

Shiro looked around. "We need to get out. Quick."

"What do you mean, we?" Lyn asked.

"You're free to stay here of course. But I wouldn't want to be talking to Dalip if I were you. You're a loose end." Shiro ran across the apartment to the window he'd climbed through when he'd first come in here. The garden below was empty.

Someone banged on the door. "Lyn Goyata, open up!"

Shiro swung a leg over the window sill. He extended his hand towards Lyn. "Coming? Or do you want to find out what they want?"

The person banged again, louder this time. "City guard. We are looking for a fugitive."

Lyn grabbed a coat and ran over to the window. Shiro jumped to the tree and clambered down, Lyn following behind. They clambered over the back fence and ran to the house at the back of Lyn's apartment. There, Shiro knocked on the back door. A shout went up behind them, they had been spotted. Shiro glanced over his shoulder. A guard hung out of the window and was pointing at them.

A confused looking man opened the back door. "Hey! Why are you here?"

"Thank you," Lyn said. She pushed past him and made her way through his house. Shiro followed on her heels. They burst out in to the street.

"Where to?" Shiro asked.

"I don't know." Lyn looked like a deer about to be jumped by a bear.

"What's the closest gate?" Shiro asked.

"The westward gate."

"We're going there then." Shiro pulled Lyn down the street. He took the first right down a small alley and they soon were lost in the warren of streets around the fish market.

They kept taking random right and left turns, avoiding the larger streets, always moving in a roughly western direction. It was mid-morning when they paused for a breath. There was no sound of pursuit. Shiro leaned against a nearby house, catching his breath. "I'm sorry I got you in to this," he said. "I never thought they would know about you."

Lyn stood with her hands on her sides, drawing in large gasps of air. "Damn you. Damn you for getting me in to this. And damn them for everything they did to Poshu."

"You don't have to tag along. Go home."

"And then what?" She looked at him with hard eyes. "You said it yourself; I'm a loose end. You think they'll just forget about me?"

Shiro shook his head. "I'm sorry," he repeated.

"I have no choice. I can't go home anymore. I'm leaving the city. I guess my best bet is to go with you to these lords of Nan."

"I'll help you in any way I can. I'll make it up to you some-how." Shiro started walking again.

"Wait," Lyn said.

Shiro turned around and raised an eyebrow at her.

"Are you sure the westward gate is the best choice?"

"It's closest you said. And we need to get out of the city fast."

"Yes, but if they guessed they would find you at my place, wouldn't they also think to look at the fastest way out of the city?"

Shiro nodded. "What do you propose then?"

Lyn thought for a while. "There's the infirmary gate."

"But that is right next to the Forbidden City."

"Yes, which is one of the reasons they won't look for us there. Also, it's smaller and a lot less well guarded then most of the other gates."

"Very well, lead the way."

They set off again in the other direction, towards the Forbidden City.

THE INFIRMARY GATE was a smaller gatehouse on the North-Eastern side of the city. Shiro and Lyn stood in a small alley, looking at it from a distance. It was just past midday. Three guards lounged on the side of the street, keeping half an eye on the different travelers walking past. Mainly people on foot used the infirmary gate. It was too narrow for horse-drawn carts to get through and it was far from most markets around the city. The few shops around were supplied by hand cart or donkey.

"How do we approach this?" Shiro asked.

"I'm not sure." Lyn said. "We don't know if they are looking for us or what they've been told."

Shiro looked around. An idea came to his head when he saw an empty bottle behind him. "We need to distract them," he said. He picked up the bottle and rubbed it clean on his sleeve. "If they're looking for us, then they are looking for two fugitives trying to sneak out of the city. What if we show them something else?"

"What do you have in mind?"

Shiro held up the empty bottle. "They will not look twice at a drunk couple staggering out of the gate."

Lyn looked doubtful. "I don't know about this."

"If you've got a better idea I'd love to hear it." Shiro said.

Lyn shook her head. "Fine. But don't you go getting any ideas." She pointed a warning finger at him. "I'll slap you if any hand moves where it shouldn't."

They hung their arms around each other, forming an awkward embrace. "Ready?" Shiro asked. Lyn nodded. They walked into the main street and staggered towards the gate.

The guards didn't look up as they scuffled past. They passed in to the shadowed tunnel underneath the gatehouse. The light of the sun was just a couple more steps ahead. And still the guards didn't react. Then they were through. The lands around Hinan spread out in front. A few shops and houses lay scattered along the street ahead. Behind them, fields filled with cattle and sheep dotted the landscape. Shiro breathed a sigh of relief.

"Hey," the shout Shiro had been dreading went up behind them. "Just a minute."

They turned around. One of the guards came walking over. Shiro considered his options. Their best bet would be to try and knock the guard down and then make a run for it. Hopefully they would get a good enough head start on the other guards to make it to cover somewhere and get away.

"How can we help?" Shiro asked when the guard was near them. His voice quivered. Shiro prayed the guard wouldn't notice.

"You know anything about the goings-on in the city last night?" the guard asked

"No, why?" Shiro's answer came out in a rush.

"I was just curious. You know. Someone's all worked up about something. Told us to be on the lookout for people fleeing the city and all that. You just looked like you've been awake all night and might know what's been going on."

"I heard someone broke into the Forbidden City," Lyn said. "Apparently stole something from someone important or something like that."

"Ah," the guard nodded. "So someone important forgot to lock their door."

"Yeah," Lyn said. "You know how it goes. They mess up and we've got to clean up after them."

"Yes, it's always the same. Thanks." The guard wandered back again.

Shiro and Lyn turned back towards the open fields and walked on.

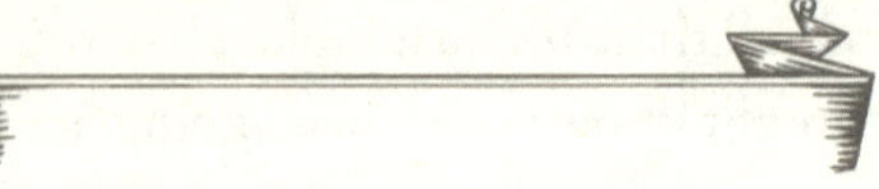

The lords of Nan

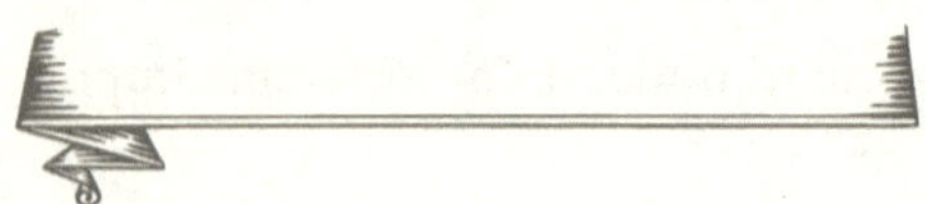

Shiro and Lyn saw the camp lying in the distance under a weak afternoon sun. They had heard rumors about the approaching lords of Nan flying the banner of the other emperor in the second town they had passed through. It seemed like the lords of Nan were taking advantage of the disarray in the empire to make a move on the capital. The rumors varied on whether they would side with the Khaganites, try to overthrow Emperor Shozun and then negotiate with the Khaganites, or if they would join forces with Emperor Shozun and bolster the defenses of Hinan.

"Are you sure they will welcome us?" Lyn asked, for probably the twentieth time on the trip.

"There's only one way to find out," Shiro answered. "But I think they will. They will definitely be interested in whatever news we bring from the Forbidden City."

"Let's go find out then. I just wish I shared your confidence."

They walked towards the encampment. Rows of tents spread out on either side of the road. Most of them were drab beige, but a few of the larger ones were brightly colored. The people around the camp were busy with cooking, carrying messages or doing drills, which made the camp look like a giant ant hill. A couple of guards spotted them from a long way off, but they were ignored like any other fugitive fleeing Hinan.

Shiro approached one of the guards wearing a pointy helmet with a guard over his nose when they reached the perimeter of the camp. The guard carried a spear taller than he was and a round shield with a lion motif. His outfit and weapons were meticulously clean. He probably hadn't seen much real action yet. "Excuse me," he said. The guard's pose changed from bored to alert. "I am Shiro of Liang. I am looking for Lord Deshi. He knows me."

The guard looked him up and down. Shiro's travel-worn outfit made him look more like a fugitive than like someone who should meet up with one of the lords. "Sure. And I am an acquaintance of the emperor; I just enjoy standing out here in the sun. Move along." He gave a nod with his head and turned back to staring down the road.

Shiro drew himself erect and assumed his most regal pose. "I actually am an acquaintance of the emperor. I came here directly from the Forbidden City with vital information for the Lords of Nan. Now, I suggest you go and tell them I have arrived. Otherwise I will just walk there myself and you can explain afterwards why you kept them waiting."

The guard jumped at Shiro's outburst. "Fine, Fine, I'll go let someone know you are here. Stay here." He waved at one of his companions. "Watch him." He pointed at Shiro. "I'll go talk to someone." He turned away and walked into the camp.

"What now?" Lyn asked.

"Now we wait," Shiro said. "He'll probably talk to his commanding officer who'll talk to someone and so on until someone decides to either admit us or turn us away."

"Doesn't sound like much of a plan."

"I know, but it's the best I have."

"Do you mind if I wander around, see if I can pick up some gossip?" Lyn asked. "I'll check back later."

"Sure. I'll be here or talking to the lords of Nan."

Lyn walked off in to the camp. Shiro decided he would be there for some time and got comfortable on the grass.

It took most of the afternoon before a lackey approached the guard Shiro had talked to, who pointed out Shiro. Lyn had dropped by a couple of times with some minor camp gossip, but currently she was away again. The lackey sniffed his nose when he saw Shiro. Then he walked over and asked "Shiro of Liang?"

Shiro nodded and got up. The lackey made a formal bow. "Please follow me Master Shiro. Lord Deshi is expecting you." He turned and set off, not looking back to see if Shiro followed.

The lackey led Shiro to a pavilion tent, striped red and yellow, which stood in the middle of the camp. A pair of soldiers guarded the entrance, and several others lounged nearby round a campfire.

"Wait here," The lackey said as they approached the tent, after which he walked in.

A moment later he reappeared and waved Shiro towards the tent. "He is ready to see you now."

Shiro walked in. The interior of the tent resembled a luxurious study in the Forbidden City, with Lord Deshi in the middle of it all. Deer skins covered the ground floor. A desk surrounded by chairs stood in the middle of it all. A closet filled with books and scrolls and another one filled with bottles stood along the edge of the tent.

Shiro gave a deep bow and waited for lord Deshi to speak.

"Shiro, well met again," lord Deshi said. "You look a bit more travel-worn than last time we met. How can I help you?"

"Lord Deshi, my humble thanks for taking the time to see me." Shiro said. "I am honored by your attention."

"They said you had some vital information from the Forbidden City for me. What message has Dalip sent you with this time?"

"I have not been sent by Grandmaster Dalip this time, my lord."

Lord Deshi raised an eyebrow at this. "Then why are you here?"

Shiro took a deep breath. "Grandmaster Dalip has made several decisions I strongly disagree with, and as a result of that I have left Grandmaster Dalip's service. I have come to offer you my services."

"So you are basically a fugitive and a traitor."

"No, my lord. Grandmaster Dalip made it very clear that he no longer requires my services."

"And all this about having information from the Forbidden City, was that just to get my attention?"

"No, my lord. I can give you information about Grandmaster Dalip's plans and the positioning of the Khaganite armies."

Lord Deshi sat behind his desk. "Out with it." He grabbed a piece of paper.

"Grandmaster Dalip is sending assassins to take out the chain of command of the Khaganite armies. He intends to slow them down and disorganize them. This will let him build up his own forces and prepare for either a siege or a counter attack."

"Assassins? That's just like Dalip, letting someone else do your dirty work." Lord Deshi placed the papers back down again and looked straight at Shiro. "And how is our beloved Grandmaster planning on getting his assassins close to the Khaganite generals? They're in the middle of an army, in case you didn't know."

Shiro looked at his feet. He and Lyn had discussed many times on the road whether or not they should mention the demons to anyone. After all, people were more likely to think they were crazy than to believe them. There was no alternative now though, except lying. "He's made a pact with a demon."

"Sorry, what?" Lord Deshi started laughing. "A demon pact, good one." He slapped the table. He calmed when he saw Shiro was not joking. "You're serious."

"Yes, my lord. I saw him make the pact."

The smile on lord Deshi's face changed to a frown when he made a connection. "So the demon that attacked us in Jaira's fort was also sent by Dalip." It was a statement. "Guards!"

The two guards came running into the tent.

Lord Deshi pointed at Shiro. "Seize that man. He's an assassin."

The guards grabbed Shiro's arms and twisted them up his back.

"Wait!" Shiro shouted. "I didn't know anything about that, I swear."

"I don't believe you," lord Deshi said. "I have no reason to trust you now, just because you say you have left Dalip's service. And I don't want a second demon rampaging through my army." He turned to the guards. "Lock him up. Search him and bring me anything he has on him that looks even a little bit out of the ordinary."

They dragged Shiro out of the tent.

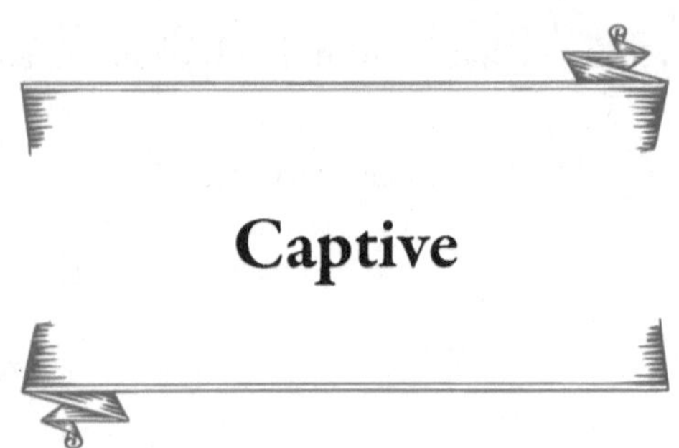

Captive

Shiro stumbled and fell when the mule stopped, exhausted from the day's walk. His guard pulled him to his feet by the rope tied to his wrists. Shiro looked up. The walls of Hinan rose up in the hazy distance. He'd made it. He had lost count of the days he had spent walking after that mule, bound hands and feet. He was somewhere in the baggage train of the army of the lords of Nan. He'd spent his days surrounded by carts carrying the tents of the soldiers. There had been one day when he had walked next to a cart filled with the rations of the commanders. The smells of sausages had made him so hungry that he had wolfed down the gruel they fed him that night.

He wondered what plans lord Deshi had for him. The lord wouldn't have gone through the trouble of dragging him all the way back to Hinan for no reason. He could have simply declared Shiro a spy and had him executed on the spot.

The guard untied Shiro from the mule and brought him to a make-shift prison enclosure containing a handful of other prisoners. He collapsed to the ground and waited for his food to be served.

He felt a pair of boots stop next to his head. He opened one of his eyes and looked up. They were armored boots. Attached to them was a burly man with a thick brown beard. A captain, judging by the insignia on his cuffs. In one of his hands he held a whip.

"Up," the man said to him.

Shiro groaned. The man nudged him with the tip of his boots. "Up. We haven't got all day."

Shiro rolled over to his stomach and pushed himself up.

"Follow." The captain walked off.

Two other soldiers fell in on either side of him. Both wielded a truncheon, discouraging him to even think of trying something funny. With no better option, Shiro stumbled after the captain.

He was led through the camp. Around him, soldiers pitched their tents for the night. The smell of stewing vegetables and bread baking made Shiro drool. They stopped at a river bordering the camp.

"Undress," the captain said.

After Shiro obliged, the two soldiers pulled buckets of water from the stream and hosed him down. Shiro gasped for breath underneath the torrent of water. They scrubbed him clean with a set of horse brushes until his skin was raw. He shivered as the wind blew over his naked body, hairs rising on his arms and legs.

One of the guards, the ugly one with the scar on his left cheek, handed him a simple outfit. "Put this on. They want you presentable."

After Shiro had dressed he was marched back across the camp, his hair still dripping from the water. They stopped at the edge of the camp closest to Hinan. A crew of soldiers was digging a trench around the camp and using the earth that came out to throw up a low earthen wall.

"What's going on?" Shiro asked.

One of the guards slapped him across his face, and Shiro stumbled back. "Quiet."

With no alternative, Shiro settled down on the ground and waited.

The sun was setting when the lords of Nan rode up. Lord Deshi rode at the front on a magnificent black stallion, dressed in a yellow and green silk shirt. Behind him rode the lords Delun and Takama. Golden rings sparkled in the last rays of the sun and all of them wore silk scarves and sashes. They sparkled like the sun setting on the river. The three lords ignored Shiro as they rode past.

Behind them came a cavalry detachment, the horses all marching in step. Each carried a banner from a different lord. Shiro was impressed by the sight. He hadn't realized how many lords supported the other emperor. A closed wagon followed behind them. It was the wagon he walked next to which had smelled of food. It was now empty, but it still smelled of sausages. A guard shoved Shiro into the wagon and locked the door behind him.

They set off towards Hinan. He would probably be used as a sign of goodwill towards Dalip or as bargaining material. Shiro settled down against the side of the wagon. At least he didn't have to walk this last leg of the trip.

Shiro peered through the window in the door when the wagon stopped. The roof of the Imperial Quarter showed over a roof in the distance. The wagon stood in an empty stable. It still smelled of horse manure. Two guards sat just inside the double doors chatting.

Shiro guessed the lords of Nan had entered the Imperial Quarter to see Dalip with most of their entourage. Only the two guards who had driven the wagon were still around. Shiro settled in, wondering what was happening inside and what fate for him they would come up with.

A voice near the door made him look up. He saw Ray standing in the doorway, talking to the guards. Ray wore a servant's outfit, carrying a tray. He handed something from the tray to the guards and then walked over to the wagon.

"Hi," he said by way of welcome. "Dalip guessed you would probably be hungry and asked me to bring you some food." Ray slid the tray through the gap between the bottom of the door and the floor.

Shiro searched for something to say. This was not what he had expected. "Is he not mad that I left?"

"No, not at all. He is just sorry about how things played out."

"Sorry?"

"Yes, those were his words." Ray pushed the tray a bit further. "Look, I've got to go again, before those two start asking too many questions. I just want to say I'm sorry too, about everything." Ray turned around and walked out. He waved to the two guards and disappeared out the door.

Shiro sat staring at the food. There was a dish of mutton in spiced gravy, some baked vegetables and a bowl of rice. The smell made his mouth water. He wondered what was going on. He poked with a finger at the food. Nothing happened. He shrugged and tried a bite of the mutton. It tasted as good as it smelled. He dumped some rice in the bowl of mutton gravy, picked up the bowl and shoveled some food in to his mouth. It was warm and heartening and savory and it reminded him of winter meals at his parents' house.

He reveled in the mouthful. For his next bite, he tried to decide between more of the mutton or the vegetables. He looked down at the tray. A black, shimmering inlay in the tray sat underneath the bowls. He picked up the bowl of vegetables and saw that a black, five-pointed star had been set in the middle of the tray. Shocked, he dropped the bowl of mutton he held in his hand, splashing gravy all over the floor of the wagon. He grabbed the tray and threw it out of the wagon.

The two guards looked up to see what he was up to. "Get away!" Shiro yelled at them. "It's not safe!"

The two guards stood up, and grabbed their short swords. One of them walked over to the tray Shiro had thrown out of the wagon.

"What's going on?" he asked Shiro. "What's wrong with the food?"

"No, it's not the food." Shiro said. "It's the tray."

The guard looked at the tray in his hand. He turned it over to look at it from all angles. He then chucked it over his shoulder. "Quiet you," he said to Shiro. "Don't you go creating trouble." He turned and walked back to his companion.

Shiro grabbed the bars of the window in the wagon door. He looked at where the tray had dropped. A thin wisp of black smoke rose from the stone. The strands coalesced. They grew thicker and outlined a man shape. The smoke slowly resolved into a demon. Its arms reached to the ground, knuckles resting on the floor. Its mouth sported a row of pointed teeth. It sniffed the air with a short, stubby nose.

"Watch out!" Shiro yelled.

The guards turned around. The demon locked its gaze on the closest guard and crossed the distance in a single bound. He landed on the guard's chest. The guard crashed to the ground with a sickening crunch. The other guard was fumbling to get his sword out of its scabbard when the demon rose up and turned towards him.

Shiro scrambled back in the wagon into a corner. He crouched down and hugged himself, hiding his head against his knees. The second guard gave a short scream, followed by sniffing from the demon. From the sound Shiro guessed that the demon rummaged around the wagon.

Silence descended on the stable. Shiro sat in his corner, counting in his head to calm himself. When he reached two hundred and still didn't hear anything, he raised his head. He crawled to the wagon door and peered out. There was no one there. The bodies of the guards were gone. Only the dropped sword of one of the guards and some scattered straw gave any indication something had happened there.

Shiro tried the wagon door. It was still locked. There lay nothing nearby which could help him open the lock. He slid to the wagon floor and sighed. If he couldn't get out then how would he explain any of this?

A noise at the stable door made him look up. "Lyn." Lyn's head was tucked around the door and looking in. "What are you doing here?"

"You look like you've seen a ghost, are you all right?" She walked towards the wagon. "I saw Ray come out of here, so I thought I'd take a look."

"How? Why?" Shiro stammered. "Never mind. I first need to get out of here. We can catch up later."

Lyn tried the wagon door, and like Shiro earlier found it locked. "Now what?" she asked.

"The sword, quick, get the sword." Shiro pointed at the sword the guard had dropped.

Lyn grabbed the sword, ran back and hacked away at the lock. The result was a lot of noise and some dents in the metal around the lock. "It's no use," she said. "At this rate, all we'll achieve is that someone will come to check what all the noise is about." She dropped her arms to her side.

"Give me the sword." Shiro stuck his arm through the bars of the window.

After Lyn had handed him the sword he stepped back and examined the hinges of the door. He hacked away at the bottom one, sending wood chips flying all over the place. The wooden plank gave way to the onslaught until Shiro could kick the hinge loose. "Come, pull," he said to Lyn.

Together they worked at the bottom of the door until a small gap appeared. Shiro slid on his stomach and wriggled through the gap. Finally, he stood outside the wagon next to Lyn. "Time to go," he said to Lyn and ran to the door. She followed behind.

Together they peeked out the door. It was full dark outside. "How did you get in here?" Shiro asked Lyn.

"Poshu and me, we used to sneak in and out of the Forbidden City a lot. Follow me, I'll show you a route." Lyn set off down the road at the back of the Imperial Quarter at a jog.

They jogged the first several streets away from the stable, Shiro following on Lyn's heels. She seemed sure of where she was going. She followed the narrow streets through the Forbidden City, aiming for the Western side. The administrative offices that kept the empire running had a haunted, empty look as they passed them. Here and there a light still burned in an apartment.

Lyn stopped in an alley next to the imperial kitchens. A stack of knee-high barrels stood against the wall. She turned to Shiro. "The kitchens have a small back entrance so they can move goods in and out of the Imperial City without all the hassle at the gates. Useful for when the emperor wants a dessert quick."

She walked to the stack and started knocking on the different barrels. "What are you doing?" Shiro asked.

"Shhh," Lyn waved her hand at Shiro.

She seemed satisfied with a specific barrel, picked it up and handed it to Shiro. "Take that," she said. The barrel was empty. "Follow me, and pretend you belong here and know what you're doing." She marched off to the entrance of the kitchens.

Shiro felt he had no choice but to follow. He grabbed the barrel in a bear hug and walked to Lyn who held the door open.

The inside of the kitchens was a beehive of activity. On a workbench in the corner two kitchen hands in white aprons kneaded dough for tomorrow's bread. On the other side, cooks walked amongst pots and pans and shouted orders and responses. Apparently, the lords of Nan were getting the full formal imperial treatment.

Lyn stuck her nose in the air and marched straight through the kitchen to a door behind the kitchen hands. Shiro shuffled after her.

The door led in to a small courtyard. At the far end an arched gate led through the wall out of the Forbidden City. No one paid them any attention as they walked out and in to the streets of Hinan.

Shiro set the barrel aside once they were through and let out a long sigh. They had gotten out. He was free again.

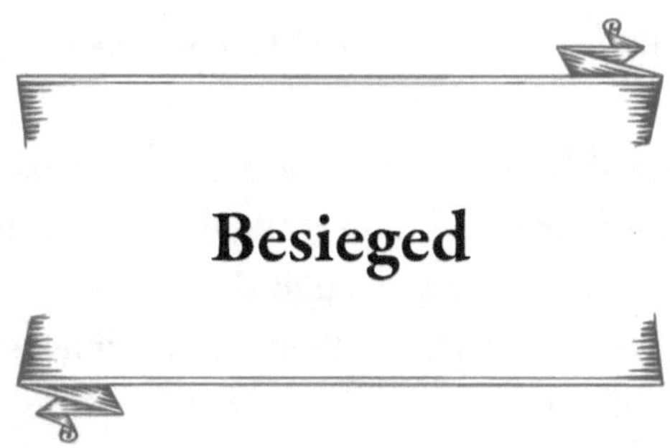

Besieged

They were sitting in Lyn's apartment. They had wandered through Hinan for most of the night constantly checking no one was following them. Finally they had ended up in Lyn's apartment. It was a mess. The guards had kicked in the door and ransacked the place, looking for any information about their plans. The table and chairs were overturned and clothes lay everywhere.

"What's next for you?" Lyn asked Shiro.

"I don't know yet," Shiro answered. He stared out the window. It felt like a long time ago when he'd had climbed up the tree in the back and snuck in. "We can stay here for a while to get our bearings. Best case, Dalip will think me dead. And otherwise he'll probably not look here, right under his nose."

He looked at Lyn. She was sitting in the window sill looking down at the street below. "Why did you come for me last night?"

She stared at her hands. "I dunno." She paused. "I couldn't save Poshu. I guess I didn't want Dalip to get his hands on anyone else if I could help it."

"I'm glad you did. Thank you."

Lyn nodded at him. She hopped off the window sill and walked to the door. "I'm hungry. You stay here. I'll get us something to eat from down the road." She grabbed a coat that was lying on the floor and headed out the door.

Shiro busied himself with cleaning up the place. He gathered the clothes into a pile and straightened out the furniture. The level of noise coming through the window increased. He walked to the wall and glanced out while trying to stay out of sight. A pack of kids, aged maybe ten to fifteen, ran through the street, talking to everyone. Shiro couldn't hear what they were saying, but an elderly couple reacted panicked and a young woman hurried away at the news.

Lyn came back a short while later. "What's happening in the city?" Shiro asked.

"The Khaganate have arrived," she said. "The first of their armies can be seen from the top of the towers around the wall." She put steamed rice and grilled catfish on the table. "They'll be here by nightfall."

They ate in silence. The sweet fish covered in a tangy sauce tasted heavenly to Shiro after the prison gruel he'd had the past days. He licked his fingers after he used the last of the rice to mop up the juices from the fish.

"Should we leave the city?" Lyn asked when they had finished.

"And go where?"

"I don't know. But anywhere is probably better than a besieged city."

"Maybe we could go to Liang, to my parents. Dalip should be occupied enough the next weeks to forget about me."

"Sounds like a plan."

They packed up Lyn's few belongings and headed into the city towards the Westward gate. The streets were filled with people with the same idea, carrying their prized possessions. The going was slow. It was mid-afternoon by the time the two towers of the Westward gate came in to view, rising above the surrounding houses, grey and cold. Five different roads all met at a plaza in front of the gate, with people coming from all different directions. The plaza was packed and they could only shuffle forward.

A murmuring started near the gate and made its way through the crowd. "What's happening?" Lyn asked a woman a couple of rows in front of her.

"Apparently the emperor has decreed there's an exit tax of two coppers," the woman said. "If you can't pay then you're taken to the Forbidden City to work for it in service of the emperor."

"Thanks." Lyn rummaged through her pockets and dug up a bunch of small coins. "We've got enough to get out," she said to Shiro.

"It's weird." Shiro ran a hand through his hair. "Why would we suddenly need to pay to get out?"

"I dunno," Lyn said. "Maybe the emperor needs money."

"That doesn't make sense. Two coppers is nothing. If he wanted money the amount would have been higher." Shiro tried to place himself in Dalip's shoes. "It's about the people."

"What do you mean?"

"He wouldn't dare, would he?" Shiro said to himself.

Lyn smacked him in the shoulder. "Make sense, and stop talking riddles."

"You said it yourself. Even we've got enough to get out. The only people who can't pay are expendable. Like the guys in the ministry, but even more so."

"And?"

"And I can think of only one reason why Dalip wants cart-loads full of expendable people," Shiro said. "He's planning on summoning a whole lot of demons to stop the Khaganites." Shiro paused a moment to let it sink in for Lyn.

"I've seen what one such demon can do," Shiro said. "It's not something you would wish on anyone, even your worst enemy. We've got to stop him."

"That's ridiculous." Lyn shook her head.

"If we don't then there will be a crowd of demons running through the streets tonight. I can't let that happen."

"How were you planning on stopping it?"

"We need to take out Dalip. When he's busy with the ritual in the cavern underneath the Imperial Quarter he'll be too occupied to notice us. With the amounts of people he wants to sacrifice we can get close enough to do what needs to be done."

"You're crazy." Lyn said.

"We're supposed to be the most civilized, the most enlightened country in the world. We can't just go sacrificing people because we think they're expendable. We might as well just surrender to the Khaganites right now, since they'd be a lot more civilized than us. You don't have to come, but I'm doing this. For the empire."

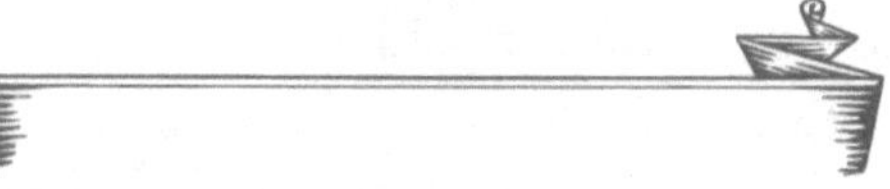

Grandmaster Dalip

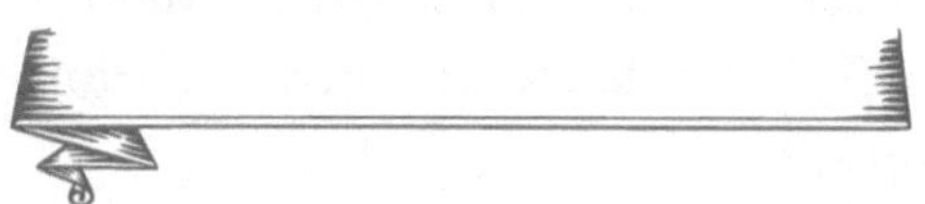

The sun was nearing the horizon when Shiro and Lyn once more stood in the Forbidden City. Lyn had known another way in. Around them, clerks walked past, going about their business. The administration of the empire never stopped, not even for a siege. Messengers weaved through the crowds, message bags slung across their backs.

The Imperial Quarter rose up before them, grey and foreboding. The light seemed sucked out of the place. The shadows were somehow deeper and darker than they had any right to be. It made the hairs on Shiro's arms stand up.

"What do you think?" he asked Lyn.

"I think any sane person would run," Lyn said. She rubbed her arms. "Let's find Dalip and get this over with, one way or another."

Shiro nodded. They walked around the Imperial Quarter, observing the place. "I don't see any guards around," Shiro said.

"Maybe they're all at the walls, getting ready for the Khaganite army."

"Could be. Let's try the side door over there."

They crossed the street to the building and tried the door to see if it was open. It groaned as it swung outward, breaking the silence around them. The hallway beyond was silent.

"You know the way," Lyn said.

"Let's try Dalip's study first." Shiro's hand went to his side where the dagger hung. It wasn't ideal for killing someone. Shiro shuddered. It would be best not to dwell on that for too long. But a bigger weapon would have stood out like a sore thumb. And Dalip needed to be taken out before he could kill all those people.

Shiro led the way through the Imperial Quarter. A single lantern hung at the end of the passage, where it took a hard left. A couple of doors offered access to the store rooms in this side of the complex.

They reached the back door to Dalip's study without running into anyone. The door slid open silently. They stepped through on to the deep carpet that covered the floor of the study. The shelves of books rose up around them.

They walked from the small back room in to the study proper. There was no one there. Shiro let out a sigh.

"If he's not here, then where can he be?" Lyn asked.

Shiro walked to Dalip's desk and leafed through the papers on it. "I'm not sure. There might be some clue around." Lyn walked in to the room and started looking at the bookshelves.

Shiro looked around. Something felt out of place. The desk was perhaps a bit messier than it usually was. But then, with so many reports on army movements and supplies, that felt normal. His eyes fell on the mantel behind Dalip's desk. "The sword!"

"What sword?" Lyn turned towards him.

Shiro pointed at the mantel. "Dalip had a ceremonial sword hanging there. It's gone."

"So he took his sword."

"If you intend to bleed a lot of people to death, how would you do it?" Shiro rushed to the door of Dalip's study. "He's already started. Come."

They walked into the atrium. It stood empty and forgotten. Shiro crossed it and walked down the corridor towards the emperor's quarters.

In the emperor's bedchamber, Shiro made straight for the fireplace. The entrance in the side was closed. He leaned his head against the mantel. He sighed. "They're more careful this time."

"There's got to be a way to open it. You search the fireplace. I'll look through the rest of the chamber."

Shiro nodded. He ran his hand over the mantle and down the sides of the fireplace. It was all smooth stone. Nothing that suggested there was anything out of the ordinary with the fireplace. But then again, any mechanism to open the entrance would be out of sight to prevent someone from accidentally opening it.

Shiro stepped into the hearth. Ash and soot whirled down as he ran his hands along the inside of the firebox. In the corner, his hand slid over a lump. He pushed and with a groan the side of the fireplace slid open.

The stairs down looked exactly like he remembered them, the single torch illuminating the steep steps and large grey blocks of stone. A deep noise came up the stairs. Dalip had indeed already started. He took the stairs two steps at a time. Lyn followed behind more slowly.

Shiro reached the treasury. The boxes and treasures had been moved aside to open a broad path to the door that led into the cavern.

Shiro started across the room. Something hit him in the back of his head and he went down face forward. "Grandmaster Dalip was right," Ray's voice came from behind him.

Shiro shook his head, trying to clear the stars that flashed before his eyes.

"I didn't believe him when he said you'd show up." Ray's voice drew closer. "But here you are."

Shiro turned around and faced Ray who towered over him. Ray held a sword in his hand. Shiro scrambled back on his hands and ass and looked for anything to block the sword. Ray advanced and raised the sword.

Suddenly, Ray arched his back and his mouth formed in a soundless scream. Then, he toppled to his knees and fell face first to the floor. A knife stuck out his back. Lyn was standing behind Ray. She looked at her hands, eyes wide in shock. "I had no choice," she said.

The noise coming through the door leading to the cavern rose. "Come," Shiro said. "We've got no time left."

The cavern door stood open. Dalip had apparently trusted Ray. Shiro headed down, more slowly this time.

The cavern below was crowded. Grandmaster Dalip stood at the altar in the center. Above him towered the demon lord. Perhaps a hundred people in rags stood between Shiro and the altar. A handful of people in robes stood between the crowd and the altar. Shiro wondered if Master Jin was again amongst them.

Dalip was already negotiating with the demon lord. "I have brought a great many in payment," he said, pointing behind him at the crowd. "It must be enough for an army."

"It is enough for a mindless horde," the demon answered. It had a glint in its eye. "If I let them loose like this they will tear up the city together with your enemies. An army needs a general to lead it."

Shiro reached the bottom of the stairs and started making his way through the crowd. The people around him stood looking at the altar with a glazed look in their eyes. They didn't move out of his way unless he shoved them hard.

"Tell me what you need," Dalip said. "I will do whatever it takes to protect the empire."

Shiro had only managed to cross half the distance. His progress halted by the press of people in front of him.

"I know. We need a powerful sacrifice." The demon lord nodded. He pointed at one of the hooded figures behind Dalip. "He is strong enough to open the portal."

Grandmaster Dalip turned around to see who the demon was pointing at. The hooded figure took a step back. "No!" the figure shouted.

"Take him," Dalip said. Two of the hooded men next to the victim grabbed his arms and dragged him to the altar. Dalip picked up his sword and walked over to the victim.

"Grandmaster," the demon said, "are you ready and willing to receive the leader for your army?" The demon leaned forward in the cloud of smoke. "Are you making this sacrifice?"

Dalip looked up at the demon. He nodded. "Yes, whatever it takes." Dalip turned back to the victim. He raised the sword. "I'm sorry," he said. "We all make sacrifices for the good of the empire."

The sword came down. Blood flowed over the altar and spread out over the five-pointed star in the ground. Dalip turned back to the demon lord. "Send your general."

The star started glowing with light, brighter and brighter, throwing shadows all across the cavern. In the smoke cloud, the demon lord started laughing. The demon lord reached through the cloud and placed a hand on either side of Dalip's face. Dalip screamed out and clawed at the hands. The demon lord dissolved in to mist and disappeared. Dalip fell to his knees.

Silence descended on the cavern. Dalip stood up. "Free at last," he said. His voice had taken on a deeper tone. He turned around to face the crowd around the altar. His eyes had changed. They had become yellow, mirroring those of the demon lord.

He looked down at the hooded figures around the altar. "Kill them." He pointed at the crowd around the cavern. "Make their blood flow to release your army."

Shiro turned back towards the exit. He scrambled through the crowd. Going back was as slow as moving in had been. Lyn was waiting for him at the bottom of the stairs.

"We've got to get out of here!" Shiro glanced over his shoulder to where the acolytes were dragging people towards the altar. "We're about to get overrun by demons. There's nothing we can do here." He pushed Lyn towards the stairs. Near the altar, the first demon appeared through the smoke portal.

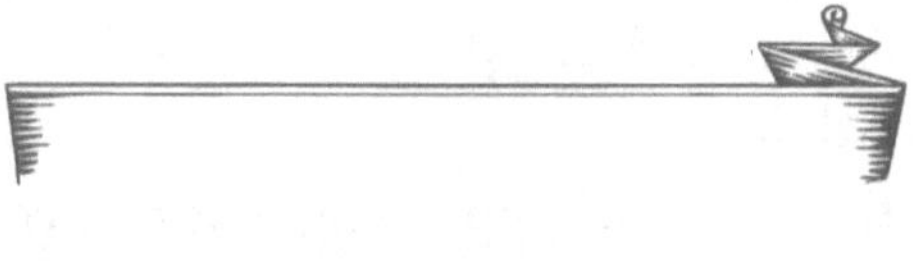

Demons

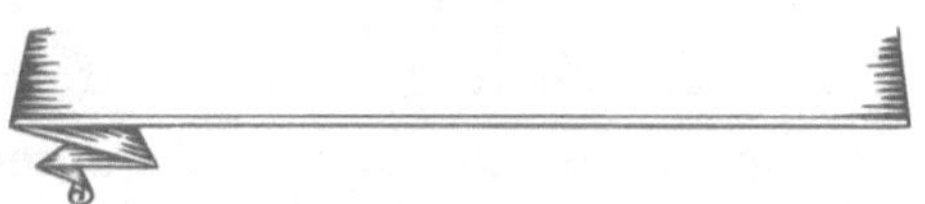

Shiro fled up the stairs. Below in the cavern behind him a roar swelled until Shiro could feel the deep notes vibrate in his stomach. He arrived in the treasury. Ray still lay where Lyn had killed him. The rest of the room passed in a blur. He arrived on Lyn's heels as she started up the second set of stairs.

The atrium was empty. Their footsteps echoed through the space as he overtook Lyn in a dash for the nearest exit. Outside, night had fallen. Shiro took the steps down in to the plaza in one leap. He looked over his shoulder to see if anything was following them and slowed down.

"Lyn," he asked, "is it me or is the Imperial Quarter giving off light?" The whole building gave off a pale white light.

Lyn arrived at his side and looked around "What do you think it means?"

A screech like someone scraping a knife across a slate, went up inside the palace.

"I don't know, and I don't want to find out. Come on." Shiro turned and ran across the plaza, down the main thoroughfare towards the Plaza of the Five Dragons. Here and there, people stood staring at the Imperial Quarter in wonder. The army camp of the imperial guards stood across their path out of

Forbidden City. A guard stepped in front of them as they came running towards him.

"Halt!" The guard held up his right arm in command. His left rested on the pommel of his short sword. "What's going on?"

"Look," Lyn said. "We've got an urgent message from Grandmaster Dalip we need to deliver to the outer wall."

Screams went up on the road behind them.

"You don't look like no messengers to me," the guard said. "Something funny is going on here. You're coming with me."

"Let us pass," Lyn said. "Or you can explain to Grandmaster Dalip himself why we are late."

"I've got to do no such thing, missy. I've me orders to report any funny business and I'm sticking to them."

The screams were getting closer. Shiro looked over his shoulder. The few people still on the road scattered left and right. A dark shadow sped down the road towards them.

"Look," Lyn said, still arguing with the guard, "we don't have time to stand around arguing. It's really important to let us pass."

The dark shadow resolved into a creature like a wolf, running towards them on all fours, larger than any wolf Shiro had ever seen. It stood easily to his chest. It had a long snout with fangs sticking out. Shiro grabbed Lyn's arm and pulled her to the side of the road.

"Hey!" the guard shouted, half turning towards Shiro.

Then the wolf barreled straight into the guard's chest. The wolf tore a large chunk of flesh out of the guard's throat before the soldier had even hit the ground. The wolf bounded off the guard and landed on all fours.

Another soldier came walking over to see what all the noise was about. "What the hell is that!" he shouted.

The wolf turned its head towards the second guard. It crouched, ready to pounce. The soldier started drawing his sword.

He's not going to be in time, Shiro thought. He grabbed a rock from the ground. He hurled it with all his might at the wolf and struck it in the middle of its flank.

The rock bounced off the wolf without doing any visible damage. It turned its head towards the source of this disturbance.

The delay let the soldier get out his sword and slash at the wolf's head. It yelped in pain. The soldier gave another thrust and the wolf went down. The wolf dissolved into strands of smoke when it hit the ground.

"Thanks," the soldier said as he looked over at Shiro. "What was that thing?"

"I think it's a demon," Shiro stated.

"If I hadn't just seen it disappear like that then I wouldn't have believed you. Where did it come from?"

Shiro pointed back down the road. "Grandmaster Dalip has summoned it to attack the Khaganites. But I think it's out of control."

"You don't say."

Shiro looked back at where he guessed the Imperial Quarter was. The night's sky was lit up like as if the festival of lights neared its climax. "We need to clear the road to the city walls. And fast. Otherwise a lot more people are going to get hurt."

"There's more of these things?"

"I think we're going to see a whole army of them before the night is out."

"Right, follow me." The soldier turned and strode towards the army camp.

He pointed at a couple of soldiers lounging near a cooking fire. "Get ten men and clear the road running from here to the city gates." He pointed at Shiro. "He's in charge. If he talks, obey like he's you're officer."

The soldiers stood up and stretched. One picked up the shield lying behind him.

"What are you, old ladies? Get moving, now!" The soldier commanded.

The men jumped and hurried to Shiro. How had he ended up in this position?

"Right, um," he said. "Follow me." Shiro walked back to the thoroughfare.

Another black shadow wolf charged past them. More screams went up, down the road. Shiro pointed. "Saw that? There's going to be a whole lot more of those coming down the road. They attack what's in their way. So, we've got to clear the road before any innocent people get hurt." He clapped his hands. "Come on, let's go."

The soldiers marched down the road in double time. Shiro followed their lead. They shouted at anyone near the road to get out of the way.

Another scream went up behind them.

Shiro pointed at one of the men. "You, what's your name?"

"Dao, sir."

"Dao, watch our back. If you see anything moving, anything at all, warn us."

The soldier saluted.

They continued down the road. Shiro jogged in the middle of the group of soldiers. "Get off the road!" he shouted at an elderly couple strolling down the road. "It's not safe here." His shout seemed to have an effect. The couple looked around and hurried on their way. They took the first left they could find.

"Sir," Dao called out to Shiro, "I think I saw something move back there."

"What did you see?"

"I'm not sure, sir. It was like a black shadow moving along."

"Everyone, off the road," Shiro ordered, "We're about to be overtaken by a demon."

The soldiers scrambled out of the way. A black wolf barreled past. It was soon out of sight.

After another block they came to the night market. Little stalls selling all kinds of food and trinkets spread across the central market plaza. The demon wolf that had passed them had run right through the market. A group of people stood in the central aisle around a body on the floor. As Shiro got closer he saw that it was a young woman. Half her chest had been ripped out by the demon.

"Sir," Dao's voice quivered, "Sir, what's that?"

Shiro turned around. A hulking shape as tall as the second story of the houses lining the market lurched down the street. A tremor ran through the ground with each step it took. Shiro looked around at all the people. "They'll never all get out in time. We've got to slow it down. Gather round."

The soldiers closed in. Shiro pointed at Dao and the soldier next to him. "You two, clear a path through the market. Get people out of the way, whatever it takes." Dao and the other soldier nodded and they ran off.

Shiro looked round the group of soldiers. Each of them met his eyes. "We need to distract it. Try to stay out of its reach. Just keep it occupied."

They spread out. The demon had reached the entrance to the night market. Several screams went up as people noticed the demon. Shiro ran to the left side of the monster. He grabbed a rock and hurled it at the demon. It bounced harmlessly off the demon's arm and fell to the ground.

The demon turned to look at where the rock had come from. At that moment, another rock struck its back as a soldier across from Shiro followed Shiro's example.

The demon swayed the other way. Again, another soldier threw a rock at it. And again. A rock hit the demon in the back of his head. It shook its head and swept its gaze over the night market. It fixated on one of the soldiers standing along the path through the market.

"Look out!" Shiro yelled.

The demon lunged forward, grabbed the soldier. It smashed the soldier to the ground and ripped his arm off. Satisfied, it dropped the soldier to the ground and continued through the market.

Shiro ran over and kneeled next to the soldier. The soldiers face was smashed to a pulp, his body lying limp and lifeless on the cobbled road. He placed a hand on the soldier's chest and cursed.

Shiro looked up. The other soldiers had gathered round. He spotted Dao among them. "How did you do?"

Dao ran a hand over his helmet. "We got most people out of the way. It wasn't too hard once people started noticing the demon bearing down on them."

"What's next, sir?" one of the other soldiers asked.

Shiro stood up. He pointed at the fallen soldier. "Take him back to your camp. See that he gets a proper burial."

"What about the demons?"

"I think we're too late in clearing the road after that monster. He's hard to miss," Shiro said. "I'll follow it to see what's happening." Shiro followed after the demon towards the city gates.

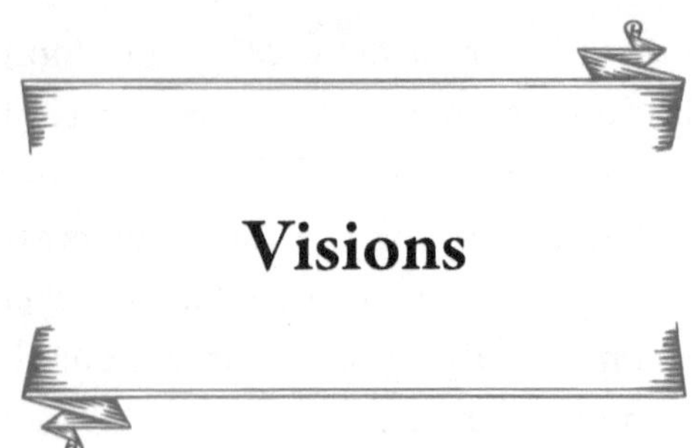

Visions

The road to the city walls was deserted as Shiro continued onwards. Here and there a body lay by the side of the road where a demon had run into an unfortunate passer-by. Several more demons in different shapes and sizes passed him on his way through the city.

The sound of thunder came from behind him when he was perhaps half way to the city wall. It swelled in volume. A black mass barreled down the road towards him. He dashed to an alleyway and crouched down just round the corner, out of sight of anyone, or anything hurtling down the street.

A legion of demons sped past the alleyway. A wall of sound slammed in to him as they passed him in a black mass of limbs and fangs. And then they were past. The pitch dropped and the sound receded as they moved away.

Shiro stood up and looked out of his alley. Down the street the last of the demons reached the city wall. The street in the direction of the Forbidden City was devoid of life.

Shiro brushed off his trousers and continued towards the city walls. Sound slowly returned. But as he progressed, Shiro realized that it wasn't the sounds of everyday city life he heard but the sounds of battle. He broke in to a run.

The great gate appeared round a corner. It stood wide open as if it had exploded outwards. The bodies of the soldiers who had been guarding the gates lay scattered around the plaza in front of the gate.

The night sky outside the walls glowed orange and yellow. He ran to the side of the gatehouse and up the stairs leading to the ramparts to get a better view of the fields outside the city.

The view from the top could have been taken directly from a painting depicting the demon realm. The Khaganite army had set up the main bulk of their camp in the flat fields across from the gates. From there, they had spread out to envelope the city.

The camp burned everywhere. Screams of the wounded and dying rang through the evening air. Here and there, clumps of soldiers had gathered together and fought against demons bearing down on them. It was always a futile effort. For each demon that was killed, two would take its place and soon the little clump of men was overrun and scattered. Horses neighed in a wild panic. A couple broke loose and scattered across the fields, away from the army.

Shiro leaned against the battlements. He felt sick at the sight.

A familiar feeling struck him. He had seen this scene before, except that it was all wrong. When he had first sat on the jade throne, posing as the emperor, he'd dreamed about standing on the wall, overseeing a war outside the city walls.

It had been a just war, heroic and honorable.

It had not been this butchery.

Tears came to his eyes as he stared out at the massacre. He dropped to his knees. This was not the empire he was proud of, the empire he had served. He needed to find a way to stop this. He needed to stop the demons overrunning the lands around them.

He pushed himself up. He turned and looked back over Hinan towards the Forbidden City. There, in the distance, he could see the tiered roof of the Imperial Quarter glow with a white, lifeless light against the darkening sky.

He would restore the empire.

Assaulting the Imperial Quarter

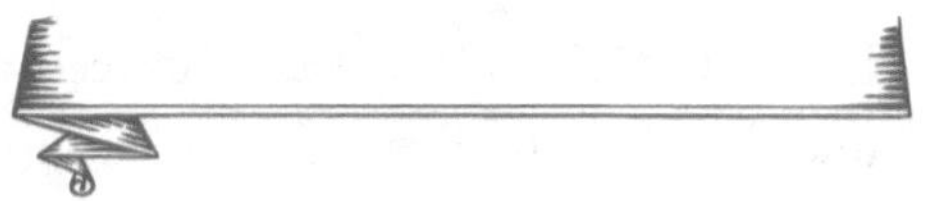

The buildings of the Forbidden City rose up ahead of Shiro. He walked towards the army camped in the Plaza of the Five Dragons. It was in disarray. Soldiers were running everywhere, they were putting on armor or gathering weapons.

Shiro grabbed one of the soldiers running past. "Who's in charge?"

"Who're you?" the soldier asked.

Shiro ignored the question. "I need a strike force, and I need it fast."

"And I need the hips of a willing woman." The soldier placed a hand on Shiro's chest and gave a shove. "Get out."

Shiro swatted the hand away. He stared the soldier directly in the eyes. "I don't care how many women you want. The emperor is in danger and I'm going to save him. In case you hadn't noticed, there's a bunch of demons running around the Forbidden City." Shiro placed his fingertips on the soldier's chest. "Unless you want more of them I suggest you find me someone in charge here."

The soldier took a step back at Shiro's outburst. "Fast!" Shiro added when the soldier didn't move fast enough.

The soldier scrambled back and ran in to the camp. Moments later he reappeared with the captain who had talked to Shiro only a short while ago.

The captain gave Shiro a salute. "I heard you need a fighting squad, sir."

Shiro nodded. "I'm no sir, but yes. We need to stop these demons. I think there's a small window of opportunity now that they're all outside the city fighting the Khaganites. But that means we need to move fast."

"Yes, sir." The captain gave another salute. "We'll assemble a squad and be ready in fifteen minutes." He turned to the soldier next to him. "Get the men together. We'll need," he looked at Shiro "how many men do we need?"

"Twenty should do it. We need speed more than numbers."

"Right." The captain turned back to the soldier. "Get thirty men from the tiger division and have them here as fast as you can." At a look from Shiro the captain smiled. "I believe in using overwhelming force, if possible."

The soldier ran off. The captain stuck out his hand to Shiro. "I'm captain Feng." Shiro took his hand. "Where are we going?" he asked.

"I'm Shiro. And we're heading to the Imperial Quarter. That's were these demons are coming from, so that's where we need to be."

Captain Feng waved over a soldier. "Get me a sword and a set of armor for this man," he said, pointing at Shiro.

The first soldier for the squad came walking up to them moments later. He was still strapping his sword belt to his waist as he came towards them. By the time Shiro had donned his armor, the other soldiers had arrived in ones and twos. They were a motley group. The shortest of them came to Shiro's shoulder and was as broad as he was tall. The tallest of them could look over Shiro's head. All of them wore a lamellar breastplate and skirt, with alternating orange and black scales, and had a short sword strapped to their belt. A variety of helmets sat on their heads.

Captain Feng counted heads. "We're ready, sir. Lead the way."

Shiro headed towards the Imperial Quarter, with Captain Feng at his side and the thirty soldiers around and behind him. Shiro started talking to take his mind of what lay ahead. "We need to get in to the Imperial Quarter," he said. "Grandmaster Dalip somehow opened a portal that let the demons in. We need to close it." He had no idea how to close the portal, but he would worry about that part when it came to it.

The Imperial Quarter appeared round a bend. The white glow had subsided. If Shiro ignored the destroyed gates at the top of the stairs, then it looked almost like it had the first time he'd seen it.

Silence hung over the plaza around the Imperial Quarter. The soldiers spread out on either side of Shiro. Their gazes swiveled over the plaza. Shiro nervously fingered the sword hilt at his waist.

Shiro hesitated when they arrived at the bottom of the stairs leading up to the Imperial Quarter. The atrium inside was dark and empty. The soldiers looked at Shiro and waited. He let out a sigh and nodded.

Fifteen soldiers sprinted past Shiro up the stairs and in to the building. Shiro followed with more trepidation. The soldiers had spread out across the atrium, eyeing the different entrances.

"Where next?" captain Feng asked.

Shiro pointed. "The entrance to the cavern is that way. Through the imperial bedchamber."

Captain Feng gave a nod and they set off towards the stairs leading down to the storage room. The soldiers flowed around them like a pack of lions herding prey.

At the top of the stairs Shiro stopped. "After this first flight of stairs we come to the imperial treasury. The next set of stairs leading down is on the other side of the room. Our goal is in the center of the cavern. Don't believe anything you see there. I'm not sure what we'll come across on our way down, so be careful."

The first soldiers headed down. Captain Feng was the fifth to head down the stairs and Shiro followed on his heels.

The cavern below was silent as Shiro descended the second stair. He gagged at the sight spread out before him. Bones lay scattered across the cavern floor. It smelled of blood and of human excrement. The altar was black and red from dried blood. The smoke portal hung intact above it. A lone figure stood looking at the portal, a sword in hand, its tip resting on the floor.

The soldiers spread out at the base of the stairs, forming a half circle with Shiro and Captain Feng behind them.

The figure turned. It was Grandmaster Dalip. "I need your help, captain," he said. "I need five men to help close the portal."

Captain Feng hesitated. The two men closest to him took a step towards the altar.

"Don't listen to him," Shiro said. "He's not himself."

"Don't listen to this guy," Dalip said. "He's assassinated the emperor and wants to do the same to me."

The soldiers around Shiro looked back at him. They took a step away from Shiro, creating slightly more distance between them and him.

"No, he's the enemy," Shiro said. "Get him."

"Hurry," Dalip said. "We haven't got time to argue. We've got to move fast. Come, I command you as Grandmaster of the empire."

Captain Feng nodded. Five men walked forward to the altar. Dalip beckoned them over and motioned them towards the portal. When the last one of them passed Dalip, the Grandmaster raised the sword and took off the head of the closest soldier in a single swipe. The other soldiers turned towards Dalip in surprise. Dalip beheaded them before they could react.

When the blood of the soldiers flowed over the five pointed star in the ground it started glowing again.

"Watch out!" Shiro shouted. "We're getting company."

Two large demons jumped out of the portal, one after the other. One had the head of an ape, round and with a stubby nose. The other sported the beak of a bird. Dalip pointed towards Shiro and the soldiers and the demons turned towards them. The ape let out a roar and the two demons ran towards the group.

"Spread formation," Captain Feng bellowed. "Surround them and take them down one stab at a time."

Shiro fumbled to draw his sword.

"How do we close the portal?" Feng asked Shiro.

Shiro searched for an answer. He needed to give the captain something. He grasped at the first thought that came to mind. "Dalip is the key. If we take him down the portal closes."

Feng nodded. He tapped three soldiers on their shoulders. "Follow me," he ordered. "We're going to take out the Grandmaster."

Shiro followed behind the soldiers. They approached Dalip with care.

Dalip looked down on them from the altar. A smile played on his lips. "You've come to sacrifice yourselves on the altar?"

Behind them, the soldiers engaged the two demons.

The soldier to Shiro's left jumped at Dalip for a quick jab with his sword. Dalip easily parried the blow and pushed the soldier back. Immediately, the soldier on Shiro's right attacked, only to be shoved back as easily.

A cry went up as one of the soldiers behind Shiro fell.

Shiro ran forward and slashed his sword at Dalip. Dalip sidestepped the swipe. He stuck out his foot, tripping Shiro, who crashed into the altar.

"Is that the best you've got," Dalip laughed. "Even your friend had more fighting spirit."

At that moment, Feng came in with a strike at Dalip's arm. Dalip tried to get out of the way, but the sword drew a long gash along his arm. Dalip cried out and staggered back.

Shiro pushed himself off the altar. He assessed their situation. The ape demon had dealt with most of the soldiers around him, only two still stood. The bird was having more trouble. It had only taken out two soldiers and it had several wounds oozing black blood in its side. But as Shiro looked, the ape demon jumped on the back of one of the soldiers around the bird and knocked over two more. Nearer to him, Dalip had killed one of the soldiers around him.

"Captain," Shiro shouted, "we've got to run! We can't win here."

Captain Feng looked up at Shiro. He nodded. "Take Shiro and get out of here," he ordered the soldier on his left. "We'll cover the retreat."

Captain Feng attacked Dalip again. The grandmaster was ready for him and parried the strike with ease. "Go!" he shouted at Shiro.

Shiro jumped down from the altar and ran across the cavern. The other two demons were between him and the exit. Both had their attention fixed on the soldiers around them. When Shiro drew near, he hacked with his sword at the bird demon's legs. It stumbled to one knee. Another soldier jumped in and pushed his sword through the demon's face.

Then Shiro was past and at the bottom of the stairs. He turned and looked around the cavern. Of the soldiers who had come with him, only seven were still standing. The rest lay dead or dying around the cavern. Near the altar, captain Feng's fight was getting desperate. The soldiers around him lay dead on the ground and Dalip was advancing in a flurry of blows. Closer at hand, another soldier went down to the ape demon. The other soldiers hurried back towards the stairs.

When Dalip eased off his attack for a second, Captain Feng turned and sprinted back to the stairs. The last few soldiers followed on his heels.

Shiro didn't linger and ran up the stairs, chased off by Dalip's laughter.

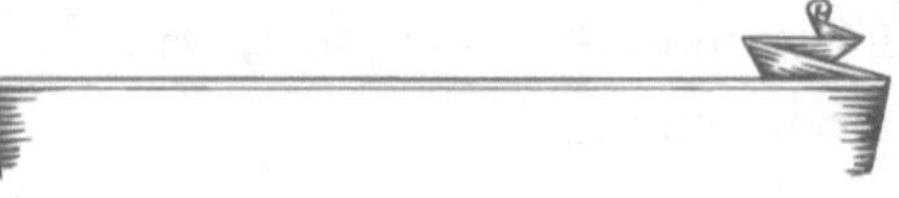

Knowledge

Shiro sat at a campfire in the army camp, staring into the flames. Night had descended on the Forbidden City. A plate of food stood untouched in front of him. He kept hearing Dalip's laughter in his mind.

Besides Captain Feng and himself, only four soldiers had made it out alive. How many of the dead soldiers had had families they would never return to? Shiro had sent them to their deaths with his reckless idea.

Someone sat down next to him. He looked up. It was Lyn.

She took up his plate of food and held it in front of him. "You've got to eat."

"What's the point?" Shiro asked. "Sooner or later we'll get eaten by demons. There's no stopping them."

"There's got to be a way."

"Don't look at me. I'm of no use."

"You're the person we have who was closest to Grandmaster Dalip. You must know something we can use." Lyn sounded desperate.

"What? You think Dalip just casually talked about how to best sacrifice people?" Shiro's voice grew heated. "Or held discussions on how to best close demon portals?"

"No, no, of course not." Lyn held up her hands defensively. "That's not what I meant at all. But he must have gotten his knowledge from somewhere. Maybe you know where to look."

Shiro shook his head and looked at his feet. He went over every meeting he'd had with Dalip in his head, searching for clues.

He pictured Dalip sitting in his office giving Shiro a mission. Shiro closed his eyes. Dalip sat behind his desk, cabinets around the walls, giving instructions to one or more guys from the ministry. Stacks of paper, filled with notes of all his meetings, covered the desk.

"His office," Shiro exclaimed.

Lyn looked at him in surprise. "What?"

"Dalip kept meticulous notes on everything in his office. It's full of all the information even remotely useful to Dalip. If he has any written records about this they're there."

"Let's go then." Lyn jumped up.

"There's only one problem. It's right in the center of the Imperial Quarter. No way we're getting in unseen."

"What we need, is a diversion." Lyn said. "Let me find captain Feng and see if I can arrange something."

HALF AN HOUR LATER, Shiro once again spied on the Imperial Quarter from behind a corner. Shadows cloaked it, turning it into a black silhouette against the dark grey sky behind it. The whole area was deserted. Still, he couldn't shake the feeling of being watched.

Lyn stood next to him. A small unit of soldiers, all volunteers, hid nearby in the shadows of the building.

"You know what to do?" Lyn asked.

Shiro fidgeted with his hands. "Yes. Give me a count to five-hundred before you start."

Lyn hugged him. "Good luck," she said as she stepped back.

Shiro nodded. "You too. Don't let them catch you." Shiro looked at the soldiers. He hoped they would make it out. He was already responsible for so many deaths. He sighed. "Time to get moving."

Shiro set off at a jog down the road away from the Imperial Quarter. In his head he started counting. He took the first side street which ran parallel to the plaza. Behind him, Lyn and the soldiers would be getting ready to fake another assault on the Imperial Quarter. He went down another side street, making his way to the side entrance of the Imperial Quarter.

The assault would be noisy and straight at the main entrance of the Imperial Quarter. They would also run at the first signs of trouble. Hopefully this would draw out the demons for long enough so Shiro could find some useful information.

The Imperial Quarter appeared around a bend. Shiro heard the banging of swords and shields in the distance. Lyn had started her plan.

Shiro dashed across the open space between the side street and the Imperial Quarter. He pressed his back against the building, trying to blend in to the shadows. The whole building vibrated against his back, like the purring of a cat. Shiro edged along the wall to the side entrance.

He listened at the door. He heard vague noises of people shouting, coming from deep inside the building. Shiro hoped that Lyn would be able to outrun the demons once they started following her. Nearby, everything seemed silent. He laid his hand on the doorknob and hesitated in opening it. Come on, he thought to himself, if Lyn can attempt to outrun a group of angry demons then you can sneak into a study.

He counted to three in his head, turned the doorknob and eased the door open, trying not to make a sound. He squeezed through the gap as soon as it was wide enough. The hallway beyond was dark and empty. The noises from the soldiers were a lot clearer now. Somewhere in the distance metal struck against metal.

Shiro tiptoed onward and peered round the corner. Nothing moved. The shouting of the soldiers increased. They had probably run into demons and were getting out. The entrance to Dalip's study appeared around a corner.

Shiro crouched down and watched the door. This was the tricky part, Shiro thought. His gut feeling said that Dalip would protect his study. And anyone protecting it would most likely be there. He watched and waited.

All different kinds of demons ran through Shiro's mind, each more horrific than the last. Finally he imagined that a deeper black shadow was standing in the dark hallway across from Dalip's study.

Shiro shook his head, dispelling the images of demons. He returned to watching the hallway. The darker patch of shadows was still there. It stood against the wall between the pillars opposite Dalip's study. To someone coming from the atrium, it would be invisible until he was almost on top of it.

Shiro felt through his pockets. He found a small camp knife. He took it out and threw it to the far end of the hallway, where it landed with a clang.

The dark patch sprang towards the noise. There, it milled around, looking for the source of the noise. Shiro eased his sword out of its scabbard.

The shadow flowed back to the door to Dalip's study when it didn't find anything. There, it took up position in the shadows again.

Shiro focused on his breathing to stop himself from fidgeting. He counted to fifty in his head. Everything was quiet.

He snuck around the corner and pressed himself against the opposite wall. He tiptoed down the hallway until only a pillar stood between him and the demon.

He took his sword in two hands. He squeezed the grip tight to stop his hands from trembling.

Shiro spun around the pillar and swung his sword with all his might at where he guessed the demon's head would be. He felt a thud when his sword impacted something. The sword was dragged out of his grip when the demon fell forward. Shiro had hit the demon in the middle of its face, almost taking the top off.

Shiro retrieved his sword and walked over to the study. It was unlocked. He spied around the corner of the door, but there was no one there. He entered and barred the door behind him.

Moonlight created several bright patches on the floor of the study. Shiro wondered where he should start looking. Dalip would keep anything this important close and out of sight, Shiro thought. This made the desk the obvious place to start looking.

Shiro walked over. He tried the different drawers and doors, but they were all locked. Shiro took his sword and pried open the first drawer. He took out a pile of papers and leafed through them. It was too dark to make out much, but they seemed to be about military supplies.

He would need to risk some light if he wanted to find anything useful. Shiro walked to a niche in the wall and took out a lantern. Using the flint, he struck some sparks and lit the candle within. The yellow light threw back the shadows around him and illuminated the painting of the angels founding the empire which hung next to the niche.

Shiro walked back the desk and went through the drawers, looking for anything useful. The desk was filled with paperwork detailing the everyday workings of the empire. There were reports on the expected harvest in Kaira, the size and composition of the army of the lords of Nan, the navy of the province of Naipur and so on. There was nothing out of the ordinary there.

Shiro looked around the room. There were shelves upon shelves of books and reports. He didn't have time to go through all of them. Someone, or rather, something, was bound to find the dead demon in front of the study sooner or later.

Shiro ran over to the nearest shelf and pulled off a book at random. It detailed the vegetation along the border with the Khaganate. The one he tried on the next shelf was about taxes over the past year. Shiro hurried around the room in this fashion, pulling down books here and there to see if he could discover some system which would help him direct his search or find what he was looking for.

At the far end of the room Shiro looked back. His shoulders dropped. Books were scattered across the floor. He hadn't found anything useful. Each shelf had a theme to it. But obviously, there wasn't one labelled Demon Lore.

This was hopeless. Dalip wouldn't keep information on demons on a shelf out in the open. Still, there had to be something here. But where?

Shiro raised the lamp. He noticed the painting with the angels again. It reminded him of the visions he'd had when he'd sat on the jade throne. It had the same heroic feel to it. But reality had been nothing like that vision. What if this had been the same thing, and it hadn't been angels who had saved the first emperor at all, but demons? What if someone had stumbled upon the demon portal and used it to save himself from his enemies?

On a hunch, Shiro walked over and pulled the painting off the wall. He laid it, face down, on Dalip's desk. Attached to the back of the painting was a thin, yellowed manuscript. That had to be it. Shiro pulled it off and shoved it in a pocket.

Time to get going. The room around him was a mess. Whoever came in next would know that someone had searched the room. Maybe he should tidy up a bit. He dismissed the thought. It didn't matter. It would probably be demons who came in here next anyway.

Shiro started for the door. At that moment, he heard a shout go up out in the hallway. The demon he'd slain had been found.

He looked around for an exit. Both the main door and the back door would take him into the same hallway. Something rattled the door.

He was trapped.

The hinges on the door started groaning as something shoved against the door.

Shiro looked around frantically. The windows. Shiro ran over. The street was only a handful of feet below Dalip's study.

Shiro heard a snap behind him as one of the boards of the door broke.

He took a couple of steps back, ran forward and jumped through the window. He felt little jabs of pain as hundreds of glass splinters cut any piece of exposed flesh. The he crashed into the street. He rolled as he landed and scrambled to his feet.

Without looking back he ran off, away from the Imperial Quarter as fast as possible.

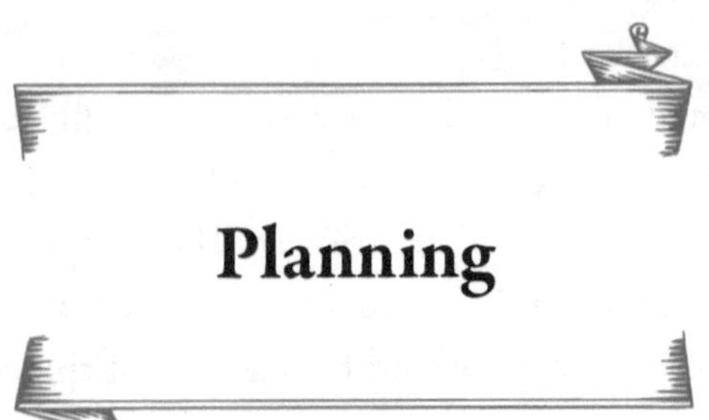

Planning

Shiro arrived back at the camp perhaps an hour later. At first, he'd run with the sounds of demons on his heels. When they had dropped away he had taken a detour through the Forbidden City to make sure nothing was following him.

The camp was silent. A couple of guards sat at the edge of the camp, their backs to a smoldering fire. Their weapons lay on the ground besides them. They nodded to him as he approached.

"Have any of the soldiers from the volunteer group returned?" Shiro asked. "Or Lyn?"

"You look like shit," one of the guards said. "Did you get a haircut from a blind barber?"

His companion scratched his beard. "Nope, none returned so far. Go get cleaned up. We'll send any who return your way."

Shiro waved in thanks and walked in to the camp through the rows of tents. He headed to the command tent in the center of the camp. Two more guards stood at attention outside it. A thin line of light shone through the tent flaps. Captain Feng would be in then. He would be of help in studying the document from Dalip's study. Assuming it contained anything useful of course.

Shiro walked in. Captain Feng sat in a low camp chair at a desk, a goblet in hand, reading some report. Two brown cow hides covered the floor. A small cot stood against the tent cloth. Feng looked up when Shiro entered.

"You're back," captain Feng said. "Were you successful?" Then he noticed Shiro's face and hands. "Are you all right? What happened?"

Shiro took out the manuscript and laid it on the desk. "I hope there's something in here."

Feng leaned forward. Shiro opened the manuscript and together they leafed through it, occasionally exchanging a comment or pointing something out.

They were three-quarters through the manuscript when Lyn staggered in. Sweat coated her face. Shiro jumped up when he saw her. "Are you all right?" She grimaced and plopped down in the chair Shiro had just left.

She took a moment to catch her breath. "We were deep into the Imperial Quarter when they jumped on us. They were faster than we thought and they already caught several of us before we made it out of the building."

"Once outside, we scattered as planned and they chased after us." She wiped her forehead with her sleeve. "I'm not sure what happened to the other groups. My group kept ahead for a long time, but they were persistent. Any time someone lagged or stumbled they were dragged down. So we split up to try our luck individually. I finally managed to lose my tail in the Northern section. From there I made my way back here. Did anyone else make it back?"

Shiro shook his head. "You're the first to come back."

She buried her face in her hands and shook her head. When she looked up again she seemed more composed. "Did you find anything?" she asked Shiro.

"Yes," Shiro held up the manuscript. "But I'm not sure if it will help us. This seems to be a source for Dalip's knowledge. It describes much of what we already guessed. How the portal is activated by blood and lets someone communicate with demons on the other side. It cautions against trusting them, since although they are bound by their agreements, they will use any room in the agreement to betray you and work to their own benefit."

"So it was all for nothing then?" Lyn's shoulders sagged. "We sacrificed good men for knowledge we already had?"

Shiro shook his head. "The only new information in the document talks about how the first emperor stumbled into the cavern with the portal. A jade pillar was the key to guiding him in to the cavern, after his defeat at Rawon. The blood from his wounds activated the portal and gave him the divine force to defeat his enemies and found the empire. He carved his throne from the jade pillar that showed him the entrance and we've been here ever since."

The three of them lapsed into silence. Shiro stared at the flame flickering in the lamp on the table. The whole empire had been built on a lie. And that lie had come back to haunt them. There was nothing more he could think of. They couldn't close the portal and they couldn't fight the demons.

Shouts from outside the tent drew him back to the present. A helmeted head appeared in the doorway. "We're under attack!" the soldier shouted. "A force from out of the Forbidden City is attacking."

Feng was already at the tent flap when Shiro moved. Lyn followed behind. Outside the camp was in disarray. Shouts went up everywhere. Soldiers burst out of their tents, half clothed, grabbing whatever weapon they could find. Feng ran towards the side of the camp facing the Forbidden City, Shiro and Lyn following behind. Closer to the edge a couple of tents burned. Men shouted in pain. The smell of burnt flesh was thick in the air.

Shiro saw the first demon. It was facing a group of soldiers wielding spears. More demons came charging at the camp.

"To me!" Captain Feng ordered. "Form a line. Keep compact."

A handful of soldiers scrambled towards Feng.

Then the wave of demons crashed into the camp. A demon charged right through two tents and swung a long arm at Feng. Feng ducked under the blow and jumped forward to stab with his sword at the demon's chest. The demon bellowed, but the wound didn't slow its next attack.

Slowly they were driven backwards.

Another demon jumped on a handful of soldiers in the next aisle between the tents. They scattered and were torn by two more demons following behind.

Captain Feng turned to Shiro and Lyn. "Get away, there's nothing you can do here."

"We can help," Shiro said.

"Take the manuscript," Feng said. "The rest of the world needs to know what's happening here."

"But it's useless." Shiro said

"Maybe someone else will find a clue." Feng shoved Shiro towards the back of the camp. "Go!"

Shiro and Lyn turned and ran.

Hiding

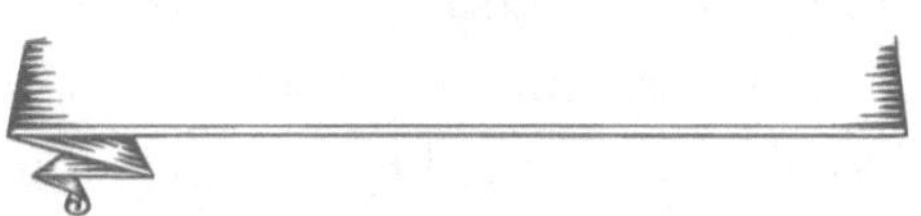

S hiro glanced around the corner. In front of them lay the east gate out of the Forbidden City. A group of demons lounged against the walls of the arched gateway.

"There's no getting out through here," Shiro said. "What about trying the exit behind the kitchens?"

"There were demons watching that earlier tonight when I ran past," Lyn said.

"I think it's safe to assume we're stuck in the Forbidden City for a while then," Shiro said.

"We can't stay here," Lyn said.

Shiro stroked his chin for a moment. "My room in the internal affairs living quarters. No one will expect us to go there or has a reason to look for us there." Shiro set off deeper in to the Forbidden City.

Lyn shrugged. "How's the food there?"

ON THEIR WAY TO SHIRO'S old room they had to hide twice for a group of demons patrolling through the streets. The living quarters themselves were dark. The door leading in hung open, its top hinge broken. Inside, the communal area was a mess. Chairs were thrown over and food lay scattered across the floor.

"I think they've been here already," Lyn said.

Shiro nodded. "Let's grab some food and head upstairs."

On the third floor, the door to Ray's room, which was the closest to the stairs, lay thrown inward. Ray's bed was overturned and blood was spattered on the wall. The other living quarters were much the same, broken into and ransacked.

By comparison Shiro's room was clean. The door lay broken on the ground, but the room had been empty, so no blood covered the walls or floor. Shiro and Lyn dragged the mattress out of the room and sat on the landing overlooking the Forbidden City. The Imperial Quarter stood across the plaza, crisp and clear. It glowed again, the pale white light made it stand out between the surrounding buildings. The rest of the Forbidden City was dark and hazy around it. They munched on the few supplies they had found in the mess hall below.

Shadows moved around the plaza. Demons were coming and going.

A memory tickled Shiro's mind. He walked over to the railing and looked down. He'd seen this scene play out the second time he'd sat on the Jade Throne. Back then it had been a sign of how the emperor cast everything around it in shadows. It had signified the divine right to rule of the emperor.

Shiro smacked his head. "The throne!"

Lyn looked up at him. "What?"

Shiro ignored her question. He took out the manuscript he'd taken from Dalip's room and leafed through it.

Lyn walked up to him and looked over his shoulder. "What are you looking for?"

"Here," Shiro pointed at the section of text describing the founding of the empire. "The first emperor rode at the head of the remains of his army, bloodied and beaten. In the distance he spied a tall green pillar and decided to make towards it. Up close it turned out to be a pillar of Jade. When the emperor touched it he had a vision of blood dripping on an altar, bringing forth an army of angels to vanquish his foes. He prayed for the divine help to aid him in his hour of need. The ground opened up and a cavern was revealed."

"He decided to investigate together with his senior officers. Inside, he found the altar from his vision. Just then, a messenger came running, the enemy army had been sighted on the horizon. They would be upon them within the hour. The emperor touched the altar, blood dripping from his arm. This brought forth the demon king, who agreed to aid the emperor for a price."

"It's a nice story," Lyn said. "But how does that help us?"

"The green pillar. It's the Jade Throne. They must have shaped it after the first emperor's victory. It is the key." Shiro jabbed the document with a finger. "It gives you visions when you sit on it. The emperor used that to open up the cavern. Perhaps we can use it to close it again."

"Do you know how?"

Shiro's shoulders sagged. "No."

He looked back at the Imperial Quarter. The image of Taizo being sacrificed crossed his mind. He'd failed then to protect his friend. If only he had known earlier what had been happening. He shook his head. He could mourn later. There had to be a way. "The first emperor managed," Shiro mumbled.

"What did you say?" Lyn asked.

"I was just talking to myself. I was saying that the first emperor managed. Maybe if we can get to the throne, then we can find out how it works. The first emperor didn't know how to use the throne either, but he still managed to do so."

"Okay," Lyn looked at him as if he was crazy. "How do you plan on getting there?" She pointed down to the plaza. "In case you'd missed it, there's an army of demons between us and the throne."

Shiro stared at the Imperial Quarter for a while. There was a coming and going of demons in the plaza in front of it. "No, we can't go in through the doors." He remembered how he'd sat on the throne, squinting against the bright sunlight coming through the skylight. "But maybe we can sneak in via the roof."

The throne room

Shiro looked through the skylight down into the throne room. It was empty except for the Jade throne. He lowered a rope through the skylight. "I'll go down first," he said to Lyn. "I'll give a short whistle when you can follow."

Shiro swung his legs over the edge. He looked down and took a deep breath. It was a long way down. He gave himself a count to three and then lowered himself. The rope turned out to be just long enough. He had to drop the last few feet to the ground. A moment later he stood next to the Jade Throne. He gave a short whistle and a moment later Lyn dropped down beside him. The throne loomed over Shiro. It vibrated very lightly, which gave the carven snakes the impression of slithering across its surface. Shiro ran a hand over the arm rest. It was warm.

Lyn touched down next to Shiro. "Now what?" she whispered.

Shiro climbed on to the throne. "Let's find out." He placed his arms on the arm rests and closed his eyes.

The feeling of being watched returned again immediately. *You again?* The thought sounded like the demon king had. *You've meddled enough.*

Shiro opened his eyes and looked at Lyn. "We've been found out, we need to go!"

"Even if we could get back up the rope again, we'd have no place left to run. See if you can do something. I'll bar the doors." Lyn ran towards the doors at the far end of the hall.

Shiro closed his eyes again and focused on the vibrating throne. He saw images of angels swarming through the Imperial Quarter. They were coming. A scraping of wood on wood was Lyn barring the doors. He pushed these thoughts aside and drew an image of the throne in his mind. The image drew closer until it filled his whole vision.

Then, his mind fell in to a void inside the throne. A thought came out of it. *You're no ruler.* This thought was different from that of the demon king. Indifferent.

No, I'm not. Shiro replied.

Something slammed against the door to the throne room.

Why are you here? It asked.

We need help.

Something crashed into the door. Shiro's eyes shot open. The beam Lyn had dragged across the doors showed a couple of splinters. Another crash and the beam showed a couple more cracks. It wouldn't last long.

Shiro closed his eyes again. *Please,* he thought. *The empire needs you.*

The throne remained silent.

The doors at the far end of the hall broke open. Lyn, who had been trying to hold them closed flew back and landed in a heap. Two demons, black as the night, strode in. They had to duck to get through the door. Behind them, Dalip walked in.

Dalip pointed a finger at Shiro. "Get off the throne."

Lyn pushed herself up. "No Shiro, don't give up."

Dalip started laughing. "You can't even do this. At least Taizo achieved something when he died." Dalip looked at the two demons. "Kill them."

At Dalip's words a knot formed in Shiro's stomach. He re-lived the image of Taizo falling, blood flowing from his neck. His hands gripped the arm rests of the Jade Throne. His heart sped up. Taizo had been sacrificed like a lamb. He would stop Dalip. He sent his mind in to the throne again. Something stirred deep within. *Close the portal,* Shiro commanded.

You're no ruler, the thought came again.

I don't care, Shiro answered. *I have been emperor. Close the portal.*

The throne gave off a pensive humming. The first demon had picked up Lyn. The other one was halfway across the throne room.

Now! Shiro commanded. Something shifted inside the portal.

"Stop him!" Dalip shouted.

The demon charging at Shiro sped up. The other demon dropped Lyn and turned towards Shiro.

The vibrating of the throne intensified. A grating sound of stone on stone came up from underneath it.

The closest demon reached the dais the throne sat on. It jumped at Shiro.

The void inside the throne closed.

The demon faded. It hit Shiro with a small thud, pushing Shiro back in the throne. Then it disappeared.

The demon in the middle of the room had disappeared as well. Near the door, Dalip turned and fled.

Shiro jumped off the throne and set off in pursuit of Dalip. The chase led them through the emperor's quarters and down to the cavern with the portal.

Dalip stopped next to the black altar. White bones were spread around him. He spoke as Shiro approached. "I can make you the greatest emperor in history. Together we can conquer the known world."

Shiro stopped halfway across the cavern. Images of himself leading a charge, besieging a city, of people bowing down to him and of people listening to his every word came to him. He could bring justice and peace to all.

He started walking forward again.

"Yes," Dalip said. "Let me aid you and guide you."

Shiro's foot struck against a skull. The image of the demon wolf jumping at the guard came to mind. "Why?" he mumbled to himself.

"What did you say?" Dalip asked.

Shiro stood at the dais of the altar. He looked up at Dalip. "Will that bring back Taizo? Or Captain Feng?"

"They were heroes. Casualties of war. We'll honor them."

"No." Shiro pointed at Dalip. "You murdered them to help yourself. It ends now."

Dalip jumped at Shiro. But with the portal closed he no longer had the supernatural speed he'd shown earlier. Shiro easily stepped aside and Dalip stumbled past him.

Dalip picked up a sword lying next to one of the skeletons on the ground. He swung it at Shiro.

Shiro took two steps back until he stood with his back to the altar. He saw the ceremonial sword Dalip had taken with him lying on the ground. He grabbed it and blocked Dalip's strike.

Dalip followed up with a couple of quick thrusts, driving Shiro back. Dalip became more aggressive with each attack.

Shiro spotted an opening. He parried the next attack from Dalip, stepped forward and punched Dalip in the face. Dalip staggered back. Shiro brought up his sword and dragged it across Dalip's chest. With a backhand swing Shiro took off Dalip's head.

Dalip's body fell forward, his head thudding next to it. Smoke rose from the body. Flakes broke off from it and drifted up in the air. The body disintegrated until only a pile of ash was left.

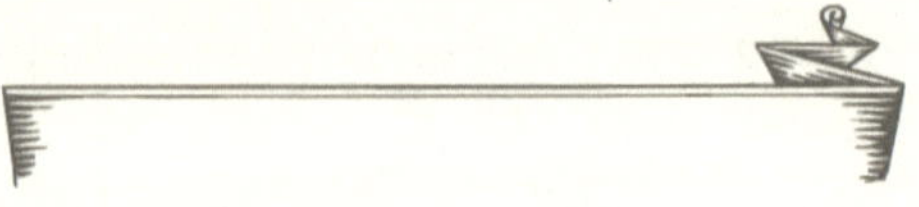

Closing doors

Shiro and Lyn stood on the top floor of the Internal Affairs living quarters, looking out over Hinan. The rising sun brought color back in to the city. Smoke rose from the central market, halfway between them and the Imperial Gate, and a few other pockets scattered around the city. Most of the city stood untouched.

"Do you think they noticed anything?" Lyn swept her arm out over the city.

"Those out in the streets last night did," Shiro said. "But no one else will believe them."

They lapsed into silence. Shiro closed his eyes and let the first rays of the sun warm his face. Out beyond the wall, a trumpet rang out in challenge to the city. Shiro opened his eyes again. A yellow dust cloud rose outside the city. An army was on the move.

"I'm guessing the other emperor has come to claim his throne," Shiro said.

Lyn nodded. "I doubt anyone will stop him."

"Everyone who mattered in the Forbidden City is dead."

"What do you think will happen next?" Lyn asked.

Shiro sighed. "We'll get a new emperor who'll claim some divine right. When he sits on the Jade Throne he'll learn about the portal from the visions. I imagine before long he'll discover how to work the portal and when the need is high enough he or one of his descendants will open it up."

"Won't the soldiers who survived last night warn him?"

"Last night will just be an example of the kind of power that's available. They will remember that and dismiss the warnings as something that happens to other people."

"So the whole thing will repeat itself," Lyn said.

Shiro nodded. "Not next year or in ten years. But it's inevitable once someone sits on the Jade Throne."

He hesitated. "Unless," Shiro said. He turned to Lyn. "What if there's no more Jade Throne?"

"What do you mean?"

"If we destroy the throne then the portal won't be found and can't be opened."

"We'll be hanged for even attempting that," Lyn said. "There's no way we can destroy it before the other emperor gets here."

"We need something explosive." Shiro thought back to Ray's story about how fireworks had once taken out half a city block. "I know of a way. Follow me."

Shiro set off down the stairs. Lyn, after a short hesitation, followed behind. Shiro led them through the abandoned Forbidden City to the Pavilion of Tranquility, which held the fireworks. They made several trips from there to the Imperial Quarter and back, carrying crates filled with fireworks.

Down in the city a fanfare of trumpets announced that the other emperor had been welcomed into Hinan and was making his way towards the Forbidden City.

Shiro and Lyn piled the fireworks around the Jade Throne. Shiro hacked a couple of holes with his sword in the throne and poured in as much of the black powder as would fit. When all the fireworks were in place, they poured a line of black powder from the Throne room to the atrium. There, Shiro struck sparks on his sword until the trail lit up and started burning its way towards the throne.

Shiro and Lyn ran out of the Imperial Quarter. They didn't stop running until they reached the buildings on the other side of the plaza.

Trumpets sounded behind them. The other emperor had arrived in the Forbidden City and rode down the street towards the Imperial Quarter at the head of a column of mounted warriors on a snow white horse. His silk robes billowed around him. He did look the part of an emperor. Shiro and Lyn stood to the side to let the army pass.

The explosion came just as the other emperor entered the plaza in front of the Imperial Quarter. A large portion of the green tiled roof blew outward. The emperor's horse reared on his hind legs and he threw his rider. The shockwave rolling out of the building blew out the windows and knocked Shiro against the wall.

Flames came out of the Imperial Quarter when Shiro got his feet back under him.

It was over.

Thus ends Emperor

I HOPE YOU ENJOYED the read. While I'm hard at work on the next story I would greatly appreciate it if you left a review for this book. Feedback from readers is why I write these stories and I would love to read yours.

Newletter

IF YOU WANT TO KEEP informed about upcoming works and get extra's related to current works, you can subscribe to my newsletter on https://www.roderickdonatus.com/newsletter/. The current extra related to Emperor is the original epilogue to the book, which got cut during the editing process. On my website you can also find other extra's related to my writing, news related to upcoming novels and a couple of short stories.

Also by Roderick Donatus

Emperor

Watch for more at https://www.roderickdonatus.com/.

About the Author

Hi! I'm Roderick.

The first story I remember writing was a retelling of 'Little Red Riding Hood', told from the perspective of the wolf. I wrote it as a play for my hand puppets. At the time, I thought it was incredibly inventive. And it was pretty terrible. I was also 8 years old.

I never did finish that story, but I did fall in love with stories and story telling. I'm never far from a good book. And while I'll read almost anything, I have a preference for reading and writing fantasy.

After dabbling with writing stories over the years I finally sat down to write a book in 2019. And I haven't stopped yet.

When I'm not writing I spend most of my time with my wife and two daughters. Any remaining time goes to rock climbing, gardening and trying to play the guitar.

Read more at https://www.roderickdonatus.com/.

www.ingramcontent.com/pod-product-compliance
Lightning Source LLC
La Vergne TN
LVHW091458170726
843492LV00001B/249